THE GLASS HEIRESS

THE
GLASS
HEIRESS

ALICE DWYER-JOYCE

ST. MARTIN'S PRESS . NEW YORK

ISBN: 0-312-32822-2

Library of Congress Cataloging in Publication Data

Dwyer-Joyce, Alice.
    The glass heiress.

    I. Title.
PR6054.W9G5   1982   823'.914   81-52364
ISBN 0-312-32822-2   AACR2
First printed in Great Britain.

First Edition
10 9 8 7 6 5 4 3 2 1

I KNEW THEN

Magic moments caught like embers in a dying fire,
Made me long to touch the frosted gossamer of your hair,
And warm it silken to my heart.
Across my patterned life you walked,
Upsetting piece by piece,
Its shibboleths and rules,
So that my time was measured by your heart.
Your sulky mouth and heavy frown
Made me long to kiss the youth it bore.
Made each moment of my day
Conform to thoughts
Of how, why and when.
I knew I loved you then.

By Robert Dwyer-Joyce

CHAPTER ONE

Rohan

I will never forget the way his voice echoed up the broad winding staircase to where we were all at lessons with Dean Matthew Langdon in the school-room. Derrycreevy came to be a house of echoes, but even then and as far back as I remember, it held an echo.

'Hear this! Hear this! Where are my pretty chickens and their dam? Rohan is come home safe again.'

The avenue gates would be standing open to welcome him, Dinny on guard at the front steps The brass plates would be shining to match the guardsman's polish on Dinny's boots and Annie running to open the door and a clean apron on her. Michael was always somewhere around to put the car away.

So this was Ireland, now and happily, maybe fifty years behind the times.

Rohan had been out to an urgent visit to the McCarthy's cottage and they said that Father Tom had been sent for, so it must be bad. They all looked at Rohan with a question in their faces and a gleam of sadness shone in the doctor's eyes.

'She's past all suffering, thanks be to God! Have pity on the ones she's left behind to mourn her. She's out of it all now, and she was a brave woman.'

I did not understand all that went on, for I was young yet, but I knew that the sun came and went with my father and that there was a magic to him. It did not seem strange to call him 'Rohan'. My grandfather had been called 'Rohan' and

my greatgrandfather too . . . all Dr. John of Derryci :evy
House in the little town of Ballyboy. I was very proud of it,
but the Cluny family, whose lands marched with ours,
thought that our heritage was not all that out of the ordinary.
As we were medical, the Clunys were naval in tradition, back
for a great many years.

Father said that the Clunys were thin on the ground in this
generation and it was a pity, according to him. Wars killed
sailors off, but country doctors might live for ever, if they
lasted out till eighty.

At any rate, Captain Cluny of Gorse Hill House had died
of wounds after battle, leaving a widow and three sons.
These were Fergus, coming on 21 now, and his brothers,
twins aged 10. Fergus was too old to take much notice of
either us nor yet his brothers and it is best if I explain about
these twins now. They were called James and John, but they
were always hyphenated with "the sons of Zebedee" . . . and
this was because there was a Jamie Rohan and a Jackie
Rohan, my brothers. It was very confusing. Anyhow, the
Rohan children outnumbered the Cluny neighbours, who
lived across the river . . . Jackie, aged 16, Ann Catherine
(me), aged 14, Jamie aged 10, Margaret, aged 8, and Alice,
aged 2. We were always together in either of the big old
houses and Aunt Bessie in charge of us mostly. She was our
"surrogate mother", Rohan said, and I did not understand
what that meant really, only knew that she was Mother's
sister, and we were all very fond of her.

I remember that morning well, when Rohan called us
from the hall and we excused ourselves from the Dean and
slid down the banisters, landed zip . . . zip . . . zip . . . on the
carpet at Rohan's feet, and Rohan was gathering my mother
against his side and very gentle with her, for she came to his
call always like a dove.

Of course, Baby Alice was the usual responsibility, as she
had not yet been given the freedom of the banisters, but Aunt
Bessie took charge of her and we were gone from the

school-room in a rush. James-Cluny-son-of-Zebedee had the gall to try to beat me in the race, but as always, I was the first at Rohan's feet and he waiting on the hand-woven Celtic carpet, two floors down in the stone-flagged hall. Red and gold and thick to the feet it was that carpet, never to be forgotten. The Dean had taken a pinch of snuff out of what he called his anatomical snuff-box and his sneeze had scattered the neat pile of papers on his desk.

'Glory be to God. Isn't it a good thing that I'm accustomed to Visigoths?' he said to the ceiling.

Rohan was a fine strong man, six feet in height and as broad as an archer across the shoulders.

His hair was just beginning to show grey badger on the temples. Soon it might be silver. He had a look of a King of Ireland about him. Michael, his man, had it too . . . head held high and shoulders thrown back in defiance of what the world can do. For a fleeting second, as I passed the rocking horse in the schoolroom, I wondered if our faithful steed might be feeling left out of it. I had an idea that his wooden legs might be aching to gallop off after us, with his nostrils red-flared and his eyelashes flickering and as long as Fergus Cluny's. Baby Alice was the only one who played with the rocking horse these days. We had quite outgrown him and it was a sad thing. Baby Alice counted him her very own now and nobody disputed it. After all, was she not still called "Miss Baby?" Dinny, the gardener, called us all that as we grew. I had been the first 'Miss Baby' and that was when he came home from the war. He had been cruelly hurt. The priests did not like him and he was an embarrassment to the Chapel, but not to Dean Langdon. He did not go to Mass any more. He had left his faith in a stitching up of machine-gun fire. Maybe his brains had been scrambled. For a while he had thought I was the Holy Child, but the Dean said that it did not matter that I was no such thing. Dinny had been brought in to the house to see the baby and he had looked at me and I had smiled at him. They would tell you that the smile was just wind, but I had put out a hand and grasped a button on his old waistcoat. That might be just normal reflex action, I suppose, but he gave me the title of "Miss Baby" and as the children arrived, it might be Master Baby and I had lost the title. It was just one of those things that happen in every family and taken for granted. There was nothing strange in the way he guarded the front steps and was head man in the garden . . . sat in a basket chair in the kitchen, slept in the stable cottage. He was the kindest old man I ever knew.

Yet, I have wandered away from the foot of the stairs and Rohan waiting for us and there was another character for you. We never knew how Rohan might be dressed . . . pyjamas and a dressing gown, old gaberdine coat and the rain running out of him, a Father Christmas plastered with real snow, gardening clothes with clayed boots, dinner jacket with creaking shirt, black tie and patent leather shoes. When he was called out on an urgent visit, he went as he was.

At last I have come to him again, as he caught me off the end of the newel post.

'Ann Catherine. Never beaten by anything.'

He always lined us up before him and reviewed his troops to be sure we had not grown since the last time he saw us, an hour before. It was protocol. Baby Alice, having arrived down the stairs in Aunt Bessie's arms, would stagger across the stone slabs of the hall to him, to be picked up and thrown to the ceiling. My brother Jackie, being the eldest, was spokesman.

'Is Mrs. McCarthy all right, sir? Was she so bad or was it just a false alarm?'

There was the split-second frown that I had come to recognise and his voice impatient, because he had to think of a reply and it was not easy for him.

'There was nothing I could do. She's better off than any of us now and in complete happiness. Maybe the cottage will be lonely for a while, but she'll have got rid of her pain for ever now . . . no more tears. There's only joy for her from this time on.'

He switched the subject to ask us if the Dean was pumping knowledge into our heads above in the school-room and we all stood there, nodding our heads.

'All present and correct then?'

He did a very formal recount and said it seemed that we were all there, except Fergus Cluny, who was unavoidably absent.

'Ach! He doesn't come here any more' I said. 'He's nearly 21. You know well that he's joined the Navy a long time ago and he's going to be a doctor. He's grown up.'

Rohan looked at us and his eyes twinkling with fun.

'Isn't that a fine thing for the world?' he exclaimed. Fergus, the dark silent one . . . going to guard the wooden walls of England for us. Captain Cluny, his father, gave his life in the war for us and left his wife a widow, and there's not one of you children interested in learning history. Off back to the school-room, the whole pack of ye. Climb up into those grand Victorian desks and get knowledge in your heads, but let it never push out kindness and humanity!'

Aunt Bessie shooed us up the stairs like a flock of goats. The nursery floor was a warren of rooms, day nursery, night nursery, school-room, bed-rooms and most of them with bunk beds, because families had been more prolific in the old days. It was an idyllic place for children, with fire-places with club fire guards and plenty of turf to burn and coal too and cut timber from the ash trees in the wood.

Aunt Bessie ruled it all and my brother Jackie had told me that she was 'a poor relation' of Mother's. She was a Hamilton and came of aristocracy but the father had drunk them out of house and home. Aunt Bessie was the eldest child of the Hamiltons and Mother was the youngest, so Aunt Bessie was very old, Jackie had it, Rohan had taken her in out of some job she had as a governess, companion, you never know quite what, Jackie had told me, but I knew that

Jackie said more than his prayers . . . Anyhow, Aunt Bessie very skilfully delivered us all back to Dean Langdon and the school-room and the Dean got to his feet and thanked her most politely.

The grapevine of Derrycreevy had delivered a problem to the Dean, while we had been away on our trip to the hall. It had filtered through to the Dean that James-Cluny-son-of-Zebedee had been into Coyle's the butcher's yesterday, and had purchased a sheep's eye to dissect. James Cluny, S-O-Z, had decided that he was going to be a doctor like Rohan, a real doctor, not like Fergus, the naval doctor, his brother, and he wanted a sheep's eye. Then feloniously, he had put the eye in Aunt Bessie's bed . . . as a lark!!!

The trouble was that Jackie Rohan, who was due to read medicine at Trinity College, Dublin, shortly had chanced on the eye, or rather chanced on Aunt Bessie forcing James Cluny to dissect it, as per arrangements . . . calling his bluff, for she was well able for us. James Cluny had been sick, Aunt Bessie had been sick. Last of all and this was a real tragedy, Jackie Rohan had declared that if he cut hedges and ditches he'd do it, rather than medicine. Medicine was out. Medicine was kaput, if he ever had to cut up eyes.

This was a major crisis. From as long as any of us could remember. Jackie was to take Rohan's place.

'I hate blood,' Jackie said to the Dean. 'It's no good. I can't stand it.'

'It's no shame to you, Jackie Rohan. I don't think anybody likes it that much, and I find it quite difficult to eat pig's head and cabbage, for I can't help thinking of the way his snout used to snuffle at my hand, when I went to scratch his back.'

There was no time to decide any judgement for we were all invited to take lunch with Mama Cluny in Gorse Hill House over the hill. The Dean was for lunch downstairs with Father and Mother. It was time to go. I remember the way we

rushed through the kitchen on the way out of Derrycreevy.
The Dean had taken his way to the drawing room to Mother.
Baby Alice was somewhere with Aunt Bessie.

We clattered into the kitchen like foot soldiers on the
rampage. Sarah said we were like a plague of 'locusses'. I
dare say she was right. There was a plate of failed cheese
straws . . . and croutons for the Doctor's soup . . . a fresh
batch of biscuits . . . some currants and raisins lying
unguarded, for cake-making later on. We were like
man-eating savages after missionaries. We were pigs
chewing cinders. The kitchen sent us off sharpish and
reminded us to wash our hands at Gorse Hill House. You
could almost hear the sigh of relief from the whole house, as
we made our way out into the oak wood that surrounded the
old house and gave it its name . . . Derrycreevy House . . .
the house of the branching oak tree . . . the wood of the
spreading oak . . .

The day was Spring come too soon. The violets were past
but daffodils were trying to bloom, and the primroses
promising and the bluebells and the cowslips soon and
always the gorse on the hill beyond the river.

We raced past Dinny in the garden and he told us it was a
lovely day.

'It's not this time of the year at all,' he said. 'But mind ye
get there in time and behave yourselves.'

'They've got baked potatoes whole in their jackets for
dinner in the kitchen,' we told Dinny. 'And a grand cut of
beef from Coyle's and apple pie and buttered parsnips.'

We were keen observers of all that went on.

'Yirrah, God be thanked!' said Danny, but we were off
through the wood and away.

The Dean was to lecture us on the origin of Irish names
after lunch. Dair . . . an oak. We had been told to read it up.
It was the origin of the name of Derrycreevy House from the
Gaelic.

Here was the edge of the river with the salmon weir and

the rickety bridge, that we took across to the other side. In places, the bridge was not all that safe. The planks and the cables wanted to be seen to, and that was our job. We could swim like fish. If we got a ducking, what matter and after all, we had the structure worn out and there was such a thing as responsibility.

Rohan was always on at us about it.

'God knows what time I have for carpentry, but it's deep under there and Michael and Dinny are no good in the water. That rope wants renewing and the planks are out-worn. See to it.'

Rohan had turned away from us one day and told us we were a pack of lunatics, grumbled that our fine finishing schools had not improved us. Jackie and Jamie Rohan and I were all past our first term at boarding schools and we were thoroughly disillusioned by it. The Cluny twins were going to be taken for the confidence trick next term and we did not think it kind to tell them what was coming to them. The tuck box and "japes in the dorm." It was all a grown up confidence trick like Pappa Christmas, God help them! Midnight feasts! How are ye?

There was a steep hill that was a glory of gorse and it was always in bloom right enough. At the top, we pulled up short for a breather and looked down over the little town of Ballyboy . . . a typical Irish midland town, that had been by-passed by the big tourist main roads. Maybe it had been forgotten. It was untouched by time and years. I did not know that it was a fly in amber that day, but I was to learn it.

We could see the Dean's Chapel with a donkey and cart tied to the railings. By now, the Dean would be starting lunch in our dining room with Mother and Father. They would be at the mushroom soup by now. We had spied it all out in the kitchen. There was to be tenderloin of pork and apple sauce . . . devils on horseback, whatever they were and then Gaelic coffee. Given luck, the Dean might be somnolent over afternoon lessons.

Then came the leap down the other side of the hill, the breathless rush up the wide lawns to the french windows and all standing open awaiting us and the fuss about us in the hall and Mamma Cluny cuddly and smelling of what we knew as '4711' cologne. We crowded round her and hugged her and knew that she was a comfortable woman, like Peggoty in Dickens. She greeted her two red-headed twins no differently to us . . . told us if we wanted to wash we were welcome, but if we didn't feel the need, not to bother. We looked very clean to her.

We explained to her that it was a matter of form. It might upset Aunt Bessie, not to mention Annie and Sarah. She winked at us to show she understood and I hurried through the routine and rejoined her, asked her how Fergus was. She looked at me keenly and told me he was well. He always asked after me in his letters. Soon he would be home for his 'Coming of Age' party.

'Something to look forward to,' she said. 'For you and me. He always asks how you are. I told you. He says your hair "is darker than ash buds in the front of March". I was looking at you just now and I see he's right. I wish I had had a daughter to be a sister to him. He'd have liked that. What are you going to wear at the Coming of Age Party? You have no idea of such plans we have!'

In no time at all, we were sitting round the Cluny's dining table and we had a super lunch . . . melons cut like ships with orange slices for sails . . . steak and kidney pudding, potato crisps, ice cream with hot chocolate sauce.

After a decent interval, we thanked her for having us and reported to Derrycreevy school-room for lessons again. The Dean was sleepy, but so were we after the steak and kidney. It was to be the origin of names and places in Ireland and we had very little enthusiasm about it. We prepared to snooze the warm afternoon away.

'Ancient Ireland then,' commenced His Reverence and reminded us we must make an effort to keep up with the past.

It was worse than we had expected.

'Maybe ye don't comprehend anything about this house, nor yet about the Rohan heritage?' he fired off at us, like one of the ancient cannons on John's Mall.

He was a grey-haired old man, with a face like an eagle and tufty eyebrows. His clerical black was besprinkled with snuff.

'This particular part of Ireland had many oak trees in the olden days. The oak was the most plentiful of all Irish trees. DAIR it was called . . . DAIR, the oak.'

He looked at us as if we were acorns that had never sprouted and he dusted his waistcoat, took out a white handkerchief in silk, dotted with red . . . and gave his nose a prodigious blow.

'Here you all live or most of you, in a great family house, called Derrycreevy . . . the house of the branching oak trees. Why should you be thirsty for knowledge, when your sights are fixed on Mamma Cluny's steak and kidney pie, Cadbury's flaky bars and chips with everything? Still I must put up with your clodhoppery. The genitive of DAIR is DARRAGH or DARR. They put it in the end of names in the old days . . . Adare in Limerick, Clondarragh in Wexford . . . Derry . . . an oak wood. Can't ye see how this was always Derrycleevy House along the years of history . . . and always the vocation for healing? It's a most extraordinary history, as long as the town records show. There was a small community of monks hundreds of years ago and it was reputed that miracles have been done on this site. There was a hospice for the poor and needy and the sick, way back in Tudor times. Finally, we got the Rohan breed . . . and they took on one after another, all down your family tree, you Rohans, and it's up to you now to carry it on.'

The Gaelic coffee was drowsing him or maybe, he was losing himself in the past. One son to the next and always the banner of the God of Medicine, Aesculapius, the serpent entwined on the rod.

'We were talking about it over lunch below, your Mammy and your Daddy and myself . . .'

'Jackie!' he shot out sharply, so that Jackie sat up and paid attention, which he had been in no way doing.

'Jackie. You're all set for Trinity to read medicine. It was a great pity the way James Cluny got the same idea, when all he wanted was one sheep's eye from Coyle's, the butcher's. It's a fool you are James Cluny, son-of-Zebedee. I think in your child's way, you've done a terrible thing. I hope that boarding school knocks the stuffing out of you and your brother next term, for is it not possible that you've sickened Jackie Rohan of medicine and by doing that, maybe you've brought down the whole house of Rohan?'

This was one of his usual ponderous jokes, but he looked at us seriously.

'Little streams turn into great rivers in life. I get worried about this problem sometimes, for it's important to me. If you're not going to read medicine in T.C.D., Jackie, who's for Rohan's mantle?'

He cast his eye along our ranks and sighed.

'The Zebedees will end up at sea. They never escape it, even if the Press gang takes them. Ann Catherine, what about you?'

I looked at the old man from under the black silk fringe of my hair and I thought it out.

'I'd be no good, sir. Death is hard to bear, even if it's only a dog or a cat you love. I don't want to live with other people's sorrow all my days, like Tim McCarthy now, when Rohan couldn't save his wife. Life's very cruel to live.'

'But you're always ready to help, Ann Catherine. You're Rohan, himself born over again. Look what you've done for Dinny. They call it "rehabilitation" now. You put out your hand and you just born. You took the button of his waistcoat. You cried when he went away to his mean lodging in Back Lane. They'd made him a tin soldier in the war and maybe an outcast in Ballyboy, but you cried when he went away

from Derrycreevy, so he was given a room here and a seat by
the kitchen fire. I saw how this house gathered him into
itself. There was room enough for all and the garden was his
world and the front steps his sentry box. Ann Catherine,
aged about nought, you knew how to carry on tradition and
you did it too.'

Rohan had always drummed it into us about caring and
about loving your fellow man and all that. I knew that
Michael was an outcast too, but Michael was a man of great
importance to us children. He had been an orphan with
T.B., healed, but nobody wanted to know and we had a
welcome for him. He might be 'the Doctor's man' now and
see to practically everything, but to us children, he was a
gem. He could replace a smashed window pane, even down
to making the putty look aged and keep secret about it. They
were all great for nursery secrets in the kitchen.

Of course, I felt very flattered that day by the Dean's
attention and I tried to comfort him. I explained that this
sheep's eye thing was just a joke. Jackie would go to Trinity
and read medicine. Likely he'd marry a lady doctor and
come home and have children . . . a generation of doctors, all
terribly happy.

We were all very happy that day at the thought of Jackie
and his lady doctor wife and I do not think there was any fear
in us of anything the future might bring, only Dean Langdon
and perhaps he foresaw what was to come.

We were a bit fed up with 'Dair, the oak' and the oak trees
outside were filtering the heat of the sun down to the shade.
My eyes were as black as sloes and I looked at the Dean and I
thought to turn his train of thought from lessons. I remember
that day as if it were yesterday. I remember the clean cotton
blouse and the khaki shorts and sandals on bare feet.

'If I were to take up medicine,' I said, 'I'd go as a
missionary, but I'd hate the tropics and the monsoons and
the snakes and the scorpions and flies and the mosquitoes
and the creepy-crawlies . . . the big spiders . . . and hungry

children, no milk for them and dying. It would kill me too. Don't ever count on me to read medicine. I'm a hopeless case.'

This was a game we called 'diversionary activities' and the others knew it and added a few remarks, but the Dean was wise to us.

'Perhaps it would be as well, if you resumed your seat, Miss Rohan. After the lesson is over, perhaps you and I will take a walk over the river and up the hill and review the town of Ballyboy. If we do nothing else, we can have a look for the speckled trout and I'll go home by way of Sandymount Lane. We can discuss things in confidence . . .'

So I was stuck with the Dean now, but I somehow felt honoured by it. His Reverence and I lay on our stomachs on the mossy bank of the river just beside the fall, till we saw the great trout and then we were over the bridge and up the steep hill of gorse to the very top and we felt the freshness of the breeze on our faces, as we paused to survey the little town, far off below. First came the small slum of Sandymount Lane, which was a problem to the practice.

'How do you like that great boarding school of yours, Ann Catherine?'

'I hate the city, sir. It's all dustbins and dirty pavements and poor women who come to scavenge rubbish that other people throw out. There's no fields and no really green trees and we walk in what they call a crocodile, two by two. It was like heaven to come home again and I don't want to go back there any more. We all think the same and we've been wondering if we prayed very hard, if something might happen, that we had never to go away from home any more.'

After a time, I went on tersely, 'It's hell.' and the Dean was surprised, but he smiled just the same.

'Do you tell me so?' he asked me. 'Isn't that shocking? It's as well you didn't say a word to the Zebedees. They'd likely not go next term.'

He asked me who had been doing the praying and I told

him Jackie and Jamie Rohan and myself, and he told me to watch out if we were not endangering our souls. Prayers can be answered a time or two and not often enough, it's all left to God. There was a chap called W. W. Jacobs who wrote a story called 'The Monkey's Paw'. 'I'd advise you to read it, before you empty all the boarding schools in Dublin. There the Zebedees might join the prayer circle for a start . . . and if they were to refuse school, wouldn't the press gang come for them and they'd end up in the hulks?'

We had all gone to the small local school for a start, but now the time had come for us to start to migrate for our professions. At the moment, the Dean had been in charge of what he called our extra-mural studies. None of us had yet been submitted to the homesickness and the starvation and the city living, except Jackie and Jamie Rohan and myself. It was a terrible eye-opener. The food was the best you could buy, but somewhere between the kitchen and the dining room, it suffered a sea change . . . and you had to eat it, or else sit in front of it, till you did. If you didn't make your bed properly, they fined you a penny, a black mark for your house and you found your bed stripped and all the sheets and blankets on the chair. Mostly one went hungry, for it had not been the food of Ballyboy, with Sarah bringing me up a specially cooked omelette with mushrooms in it, because I might not fancy the rashers and eggs again! Oh, we were spoilt with such kindness and love. It was the same with the Clunys and the Zebedees, but as yet we had given them no warning. At the present time, Jamie Cluny was having an interval when he would eat nothing for breakfast, except a gammon rasher of Limerick ham and some scrambled egg.

'It's as well to be shot with your eyes blindfold', sighed the Dean. 'You're doing the wise thing, Honey.'

A long time Dean Langdon had appointed himself Master of Studies. I often think he might have been meant to be a father of a great many children, for he loved children so. He had been a good friend to the Clunys when the Captain was killed in 1951, and Mrs. Cluny had been left with Fergus and the Zebedees. He counted all of us his children and he had filled in the Latin and the Euclid and the English language and Lit. – the dash of Greek, so that we were not Barbarians, though we never quite understood that. God bless him! I know that he taught us how to live. Certainly, he guided my feet and I knew he loved me, thought that I was the bright one . . . saw promise in me, as if he had struck a streak of gold in a desert land. He said so, but it was just his nonsense.

He was looking at me seriously now.

'There are times when I see a great future before you, Ann Catherine. I've wondered how one child could entrap my heart the way you've done. You've got your whole future before you, gold plated. How else can it be? The easy natural thing for you to do would be to make a good marriage and fulfil the woman task . . . bear fine children for your man . . . or maybe for your house, but things never run right. When Captain Cluny died, I had this same great uneasiness that fate had some fearful foe waiting. I've got the same feeling again, when I hoped never to experience it. I have a feeling that there's something else coming down the skids of fate . . . and you're in the thick of it, and I don't know how it can come to be. I'm sorry that you don't like boarding school, for your reports were first class. Maybe I'm getting neurotic, but I scented out the demon that hit Gorse Hill House nigh ten years ago or maybe more now . . .'

We stood side by side at the top of Sandymount Lane and you could smell the turf from the chimneys and the peppery smell of the gorse. The bees were hard at work as usual, filling the air with laziness sounds and the sunshine was over all with the pepper of the gorse.

The cottages had chickens running in and out through their half doors and there were clamps of turf piled against the side of each cottage, an insurance for a hard winter.

The people of Sandymount Lane seemed happy enough, but I knew what they were in the practice. Maybe I worried aloud.

'Ach, Girleen, it's no wonder I fret about you. You're a strange character, thinking you can put right the whole world.'

He looked down at me severely and warned me that he knew everything that went on and I believed he did.

'Rohan gave you a shilling for cleaning the car last week and you went out the town to buy liquorice straps. You met Gallagher below and he spun you a tale that his children were starving. Then he drank your hard-earned cash. His family was no better off . . . worse even, for the drink gave him the ill will to beat his wife and give her two black eyes . . . and that's where your money ended. For pity's sake, don't ever do such a kind act again. Give food, not money, or *take* food to the family, so that he can't get his hands on it. If you were to give the money to Mrs. Gallagher, he would have it off her. Harden your heart, but don't ever do such a thing, or maybe you'd break mine.'

His hand came out to rest on my head and he left the warm sun on the golden shine in the black silk.

'It's not for want of trying, Ann Catherine, little Cat. Don't break your heart. Just look down below on Ballyboy town and all the broad streets leading into it. Would you just look at the new yellow traffic lines and they trying to make the cars go one way in a country, that never believed in law, nor yet order?'

The whole town hung there in the sunshine, as clear as crystal.

'Phelan's cows are going out to pasture after the milking, against the new one-way traffic system. It's the old donkey, that's leading the herd. He's the brains, always has been. Why should they walk all round the green to come to the Nuns' field? They've always gone the way he's leading them and they always will. Anyway, when you think of it, isn't it the half day and no traffic in the town at all, Thursdays?'

We looked back down towards Derrycreevy House, far, far over the heads of the branching oak trees. You could see the river further along, curving with grace, and the gleam of the water shallows a mile or so further along. On our side of the hill was Gorse Hill House and there was a climb up gracious lawns to reach the white windows, french windows, standing open. It was a gentleman's residence, very elegant with a white-pebble dash to it . . . very elegant in the old days. The Dean had just told me that he knew the fate that befell it, when Captain Cluny died, Fergus would have been about the age of the Zebedees now and the Zebedees themselves infants. Mammy Cluny had done well to keep it as it was.

I smiled at the Dean.

'The Cluny twins will be rear-admirals before they're finished. That will teach them to put a sheep's eye in poor Aunt Bessie's bed.'

'Aunt Bessie, Miss Hamilton,' the Dean said. 'There's another story for you,' but he did not tell me what.

We went down the hill, and arrived at river level, deciding we must see the trout again. He was just as big as we remembered him, in a patch of camouflage, caught in reflection by a rowan tree and its red-come-autumn berries. He slid into the mirror of the rowan and his speckles hid him. There were primroses on the bank in clumps that reflected back to us. The sun was making a glory of the ripples in the water and the weed was a cool green everglade. Near the weir was the thundering water and the long smooth fall of the salmon leap. Here was where the fish waited, who had come up for the spawning. The trout kept his exit open behind the gunmetal boulder. There was every colour when you watched that stone. He was a fine salmon trout. It might have broken your heart if you were to catch him. The Dean agreed with me. Just for now, he was King of the river. I waved my hand and made him vanish. Then the Dean was dusting off his knees and we were on our way to the gates, to see what sort of job they had done with the gold paint on the name of Derrycreevy House and if it shone equal to the polish of Rohan's gold plates.

'This is a gracious house,' the Dean said almost to himself. 'It has stood for a long time and should still stand, with the voices of the children in it and laughter. I'm always trying to tell you something above in the school-room, but I'll tell you one thing now. There's a deal of laughter here and laughter is a strong emotion. Laughter might wipe out the Slough of Despond . . . wipe the tears of people, who have lost hope. Do you know, Ann Catherine, sometimes I believe that laughter could slam the gates of hell.'

There were times when he spoke like this and mostly I could not understand him, but in time I did.

'I know if I laugh, I turn a switch and the sun comes on,' I said.

'You're coming to be a great philosopher, Little Cat,' he said and grinned at me.

Dinny had come to open the gate for his Reverence and Dinny had a lean body and white hair and soldierly bearing.

His cap was in his hands in honour of His Reverence and the Dean made conversation by asking how my studies were coming along.

'Miss Ann is the pick of the bunch, sir,' said Dinny. 'There's nothing blind to her in the learning and she walks with gentleness in her heart. If there was to be trouble, it's herself you'd go to.'

The Dean laughed at him.

'It might be a great trouble if one was to fall and cut a knee, Dinny. Is that what you meant?'

'Far more than that, sir. She could carry the weight of Derrycreevy on her own back, and glory in doing it.'

They said Dinny was strange and that he had lost his faith. The Dean would not have it. Dinny was for confession at the Dean's door every Thursday night and his Mass said after and I thought that a sure passport to heaven. Now the Dean switched the conversation on to the growing of potatoes and that was just to cut me out of real affairs. He started talking about the cultivation of potatoes with Dinny and I was excluded. Dinny put potatoes down in feathers an odd time and that cut his Reverence out and me too. Then at last the Dean fired off the question at Dinny and puzzled Dinny as much as he did me.

'Your garden is unbeatable, Dinny, but what of our little Cat here? I've taken to worrying. I'll tell you no lie. What sort of doctor would Miss Ann Catherine make, if there were no heirs to Derrycreevy only herself?'

'Of the lot of them, James Cluny, Son of Zebedee is the one sir. Leave the Rohans out of it. He was playing in the kitchen and he had to have my tonsils out and Sarah giving me the gas . . . sheep's eye or no sheep's eye. James Cluny will never sail the sea. Sarah was lepping mad at the whole pack of them and her trying to cook the dinner. The Rohans have not produced one doctor, not in this generation. That's the way it goes, your Reverence.'

There was a shadow about the Dean.

'It's what I've been thinking, but I don't understand how it could come about.' He took my face between his hands and I hoped my face was clean.

He thanked me for having him in Derrycreevy House and there was a ring of old-fashioned grandeur about it, as if I was a grown lady.

'So James Cluny is to take your crown?' he said sadly. 'I'll not believe it. Ladybird, ladybird, fly away home, if that's to be the way of it, your house is on fire. Your children are gone. All except one and that's little Ann, and she has crawled under the warming pan!'

He was not joking now and he seemed troubled. 'If it comes out awry and if Dinny's right, it may do, crawl under the warming pan and hold tight. God could never see you so wronged. Never! I give you my word on it.'

I did not know it that day, but maybe the Dean had seen it happen. He had summed it all up in the verse of a nursery rhyme.

'Ladybird! Ladybird! Flyaway home . . .'

Maybe that was to be the way it came out, I do not understand and never will but meanwhile life wound its quiet way along.

Sometimes, there were high spots in our routine, but one that was special was Fergus Cluny's Coming of Age Party. He was coming home to visit Gorse Hill House and maybe it took our minds off the subject of Mother's health. She had not been really well since the birth of Baby Alice. Alice herself was as strong as a little Kerry calf, but Mother was often not well . . . willing to lie down in the afternoon, instead of coming scavenging the fields with us or having a set of tennis. I had always considered her the strong one of her and Rohan. I had seen Rohan come to her for help with his head in his hands. It seems that I occasionally hid under the dining room table and Rohan was never done saying I had long ears. I broke in on a private session thus one day and I overheard a conversation about young Johnnie Gallagher of Sandymount Lane.

'I can't find out what ails that boy,' Rohan started and it was too late for me to get out.

'Gallagher's eldest . . . that boy is going to die, if I don't find it out. He's given up eating and I don't see why. He's dying on me. He'll die if I can't find the answer. His face is to the wall and in some silent way, he doesn't want to live any more.'

Mother was unofficial health visitor, had been for a long time, but now, maybe she was fighting for her own life. Maybe she was drowning in her own quicksands and not able to go to the help of people in grave trouble and maybe it killed her as much as anything did, this feeling of frustration.

Just for now, I could hear the laughter still in her voice even yet.

'It's time somebody nobbled Gallagher,' Mother said, and I had to lie as still as a dead mouse, for it was forbidden to eavesdrop. I just had not got out in time and now I was stuck with it.

'Gallagher will have to be stopped killing his own family with drunken cruelty. That's the answer to Johnnie. Gallagher drowned the kittens in a bucket of water some time back, but yesterday, I found out that the cat went too in a sack in the river and a stone in it. The cat was the one thing that Johnnie loved. I knew it and I was not well for a few days. When I got about again, the cat was gone and I blamed myself.'

There were tears in her voice and I hated myself for being an eavesdropper, but she went on.

'Get on with the practice, John. Leave Gallagher to me!' she said. 'Don't go striding up Sandymount Hill to beat hell out of him. I'll see him and talk to him. He just wants a bit of firmness and maybe a chance of work, so that he hasn't the time to drink his sorrows away.'

'So always I leave you to be my health visitor and spy,' he said. She laughed then and told him to be on his way.

'Leave it,' she promised. 'Johnnie will get better, you'll see.'

This all happened in the background of Fergus Cluny's Birthday Party. I got out from under the table and safe back to the nursery, where our party dresses were being fitted. There was complete chaos there and Jackie and the Zebedee twins being difficult about doing what they called 'kids stuff'. They were over-ruled by the others. The costumes were quite something . . . out of the past with a magic about them. Aunt Bessie and Sarah and Annie had created a masterpiece. It was a scene from the old days, a group dressed in ivory satin. Perhaps it was Beau Nash, with the gentlemen in tight knee breeches and flowing cravats . . . with all the grace of the days that were gone. The girls were to wear crinolines and pantalettes. Dickens himself might have seen it so, 'brave in ribbons', as he said.

All the time, I was wondering about Mother and what she intended to do about Gallagher. There was a visit to the R.C. Church of the Redemptorist Fathers to come to Ballyboy, and I toyed with the idea of going to ask them what to do. I could not see them getting worked up about a cat, but I could mention 'the demon alcohol'. Somehow I left it too late Then next day, there was a kitten in a basket in the kitchen and nobody knew a thing about it, but I guessed. The house was running over with the excitement of the big party. Nobody wanted to talk about a kitten, or to worry about it.

Annie and Sarah were scolding Mother, telling her to keep away from the Gallagher cottage. I knew well what was afoot and I was full of fear. In the kitchen, every body talked about the ball. There were to be Chinese lanterns all along the avenue to Gorse Hill House from their front gate and Mister Fergus would be home . . . better late than never.

The Derrycreevy children and the Zebedee twins were to go to the ball as a set piece. Aunt Bessie had arranged music on a recorder . . .

> 'Boys and girls come out to play
> The moon doth shine as bright as day.
> Leave your supper and leave your sleep,
> Join your playfellows in the street.
> Come with a whoop and come with a call,
> Come with a good will or come not at all.
> Up the ladder and down the wall
> A ha'penny candle will light ye all.
> You'll find milk and I'll find flour,
> And we'll have a pudding in half an hour . . .'

It was played perhaps on an old spinet, but it had such magic to it. It would fill the whole garden with the days gone by . . . jingling in rhyme, music box music . . . gone and almost forgotten, yet echoing still down the years. There was a spookiness about it, That day the whole thing started with the dress rehearsal, the knee breeches, the silk top hats, the crinolines and the minuet.

Gallagher and the drowned cat and the kittens tangled in my mind. I was supposed to be lying down, when I suddenly sat bolt upright in my bed. The kitten in the kitchen made sense and all the sending to the nursery to rest. Mother had planned to go on a crusade . . . alone. Well I knew it! It all fitted in so well and I knew that she would not take Annie or Aunt Bessie. She would go by herself. I was out of bed with no thinking. I jumped in my shorts and sandals and the high-necked wool sweater. There was the ivory satin costume waiting for me to put on, the little ivory slippers under the chair, the fan . . . later . . . much later.

I knew there was something going on in Gallagher's cottage . . . something very big . . . something that maybe nobody could alter. I went like a hare through the oaks and over the swing bridge, up the hill of gorse and there I halted. The chimneys of the Gallaghers' cottage was smoking at my feet and the hens perching on the half door as usual. I knew that Mother must come here and knew that soon she would arrive. I found a hiding place on the crest of the hill, behind a clump of gorse, where I could see and not be seen. There was no excuse for that kitten in our kitchen, only the obvious one I was counted too young to be involved, but I was involved. Age had nothing to do with it. In case Mother ran into trouble, I was there. Rohan was the last person she would ever tell, but why had she not told me? This was not a thing she must ever tackle alone. I had checked that the kitten had gone from the kitchen, so I lay behing the gorse bush and waited.

'I've come up to speak with your husband, Mrs. Gallagher.'

It was her voice . . . 'Oh, but he must see me. I insist on it. I'll come in this minute and see him, no matter what he says, if he won't step outside and see me. I'll tell him more too. If he doesn't talk to me now, he'll talk to Rohan and then to the police. I'll call on the Redemptorist Fathers and request that they see him personally, though I'm easier to deal with than they are. I count myself a friend of yours. I wonder if your man knows that I can have hell down on his head, if he doesn't play it my way. All I've done today is to bring Johnnie a kitten. A new kitten.'

It was past time that I was by her side, for Gallagher was full of drink inside on the bed. I had a terrible fear of drunken men and there were plenty in the streets of Ballyboy on a Fair Day. I got to my feet hesitantly and was taken in a Rugby tackle into the sandy earth. An arm collected me and fingers at my lips for silence and a voice that I knew, in my ear hushing me. It was Fergus Cluny, but I hardly recognised this grown-up man. How could he be in Ballyboy? He was not expected yet. There was no doubt that I was his prisoner. I had not seen him for ages . . . years. We had drifted apart, since his Dartmouth days. Always he seemed to be in one part of the world and myself in another. I would not have known him from the Dartmouth cadet. This was a near stranger . . . coming of age now and grown out of all knowledge. His voice was at my ear, telling me that he had come on an earlier train . . . had arrived in Derrycreevy and found 'a health visitor crisis'.

'Your mother had just left the kitchen with a kitten for Sandymount Lane. Annie and Sarah were in a state about it. They were of the opinion that Gallagher would murder "Marmee" and her kitten. I thought somehow I'd find you here.'

There was laughter in his whisper.

'Don't worry, I promise you that Marmee could whip Gallagher with one hand tied behind her back. I knew where to look for her and of course you'd be around . . . you always were . . .'

He tousled my hair with one hand . . .

'Don't worry about Marmee. If the worst comes to the

worst, I'll go down and kill Gallagher. Time it was seen to.'

He held my head against his shoulder to shut off the angry words from the lane, but I shifted a little and heard it all. This then was Fergus Cluny with every dream of romance, I had ever known . . .

'We don't want bloody kittens about the house,' said Gallagher and my mother was patient with him.

'Your little boy is going to die, Gallagher. Do you know that almost you've killed him? It would be an unnecessary thing to do to a child, who is your eldest son and who had inherited nothing. The old queen cat was the one thing that he had really loved and you drowned her kittens and then put her with a stone in a sack in the river. Don't think I don't know it. If that boy dies, you'll have killed him and you'll have to answer for it . . . to me and to . . . to . . . to Rohan and maybe to God.'

She was well able for Gallagher, but Fergus held me more tightly in his arms. He knew the battle that had to be fought, but he had faith in Marmee. Marmee, and that was his name for her . . . was afraid of nothing.

Mother was winning the victory. The kitten was out of the basket on the floor and Johnnie was giving it milk in a cracked saucer. Then quite suddenly, it was all over. Mother had brought food and kindness and love and caring. Fergus and I knew that we were unnecessary. I remember being very proud of her, as Fergus and I climbed to the top of the windy hill. Mother was gone and Johnnie Gallagher was out in the yard with the kitten. It was finished and decided. Mother had gone off down Sandymount Lane on her way home and there was food in the cottage and reconciliation. There was happiness, maybe, just for a while.

Meanwhile, Fergus and I stood on top of the windy hill.

'I never heard a word of what went on and neither did you,' he said. 'We were unnecessary. The lady fought her own battle. Isn't it a good day to be alive? Now we have a secret, you and I. I don't even know about the pageant set for tonight and of "Boys and girls come out to play", but if I stick about a bit, I daresay I'll find out.'

I took one frightened look at him and hared off down the hill. I got back to bed, before anybody missed me. Soon the actual preparation for the ball started and I hoped that Fergus did not think later on, that we were all tom fools with "Boys and girls come out to play".

We had pushed back the years . . . maybe had sprinkled some magic dust. The party was wonderful and quite unbelievable. We came out to play and play we did. There were Chinese lanterns lit all along the avenue of Gorse Hill House, but I've said that already. Fergus and the drowned queen puss and the Gallagher affair, and 'The Boys and girls come out to play' pageant, had all been spun in my head in a liquidiser – and mixed irretrievably. I looked at myself in the ivory satin crinoline and thought I might have been a woman grown. Surely no child of fourteen years of age? There was magic in the night.

It was impossible to fall in love at my age, with Fergus Cluny. Sensibly I diagnosed infatuation, yet the next morning, I went to the crest of the hill overlooking Sandymount Lane.

I had gone there to check up on Gallagher's cottage and Fergus had the same idea. I was rather surprised that Mother was not there too. Fergus greeted me with the good news that all was well in the cottage and said that his party had been something to remember for ever.

'I'm sorry to hear that your mother isn't well,' he said, and that was the first I had heard of it. He saw the look of alarm in my face and assured me that it was nothing much.

'Don't look so frightened, Little Cat,' he said. 'They have it at home that she had a pain in her chest . . . got to stay in bed for a day or two.'

He sat himself down on a little mound, his hands clasped about his knees and smiled up at me.

'There's a grape-vine between the two houses. There's

nothing blind to anybody. We even have it in Gorse Hill that
Rohan is planning a holiday, but not quite yet. "When she's
fit for it," they say and my Zebedee brothers are wild with
excitement about it, for Rohan has decided that they'll be
invited too. it's to be something exotic . . . a special holiday
to counteract the stress of Ballyboy. Stress, I ask you! It's not
aimed at Galway or Kilkee nor yet Greystones. If I were to
ask you to guess, you might say Nombre de Dios Bay and
that's near enough. Rohan has decided to go to some place
on the East Coast of England and he's to book a four-star
hotel, so that Marmee can lie in a private suite and have life
pass her by. He wants life to pass her by! I sometimes wonder
what sense he has to plan such a thing and then to arrange
that everybody tags along too . . . my Zebedee brothers and
the rest of the gang and Annie and Aunt Bessie . . . and the
whole nursery. She'd have been better on a coral island, just
Rohan and herself . . . I hope she'll soon be better, but
Marmee will never let life pass her by.'

Fergus was away back to medical school almost at once,
and Marmee had six weeks in bed and all of us mighty
subdued. Marmee never stayed in bed unless she was having
one of us, but we all built up the idea of the great holiday.
One day Father lined us up and put the situation to us.
Mother had had a clot on her heart and it was a common
enough complaint nowadays. It was a hazard of stress, so
there must be no more stress. I think that Mother might have
been better with Himself alone and they on the silver sands
of the Atlantic, watching the tides ebb and flow. If that was
what she wanted, I knew he had made a wrong choice. Who
can judge if it was Rohan's fault, the whole thing? God have
mercy on us all! Who can ever say? Who can judge? I wished
that Fergus was still in Gorse Hill, for I knew that I could
talk to him. I had seen the small train chug out from
Ballyboy station platform the night after the Birthday Ball
. . . he was gone and suddenly I had known my world empty,
not even guessed how empty it was to become.

Mother was content to lie quiet and we were on our best behaviour. We built ourselves up with the dream of the wonderful holiday to come.

'In this hotel we've booked, Marmee, you can lie in your private suite and nobody can disturb you. You can see life outside your window. We'll come back all the time and tell you our adventures and the journey will be nothing . . . down to Shannon in the car and then a plane right to Seaport and a taxi to the hotel.'

Seaport was a children's paradise with all the fun of the fair. Aunt Bessie would be with us and Annie too, specially to take care of Mother. Sarah and Dinny and Michael would be in charge of Derrycreevy. The neighbouring doctor was taking on the practice. Nothing could go wrong . . .

When the time came, we let none of the excitement flood against Mother. As I said, it was a short drive to Shannon and just a step across the Irish Sea. We came down out of the skies to the edge of Seaport and from there into a taxi to the Hotel. We were astonished that Seaport was a city and no town. The promenade went on for miles and you could walk on the heads of the people, or so it seemed to our unsophistication. The sea-front was one excitement after another . . . the pier, the band-stand, the Winter Garden, the boating lake . . . a theatre, a music hall, a cinema, that had two shows on at the same time. On the side away from the sea were the chinese take-aways, the bingo halls, the restaurants, the fish and chip shops, the Palace of Fun, the arcades. There were sad-looking horses drawing victorias on the road and donkeys down on the sands . . . deck chairs too. There was a great fun fair with hobby horses and swing boats and roller coasters . . . and stalls of all kinds. We never imagined such a place existed. It was so much better than Dublin and the boarding schools that awaited. The hotel was a feudal castle with page boys to cope with all the baggage and make a great fuss of Madame. We had rooms on the first floor and our own private sitting room, with a piano . . . a day bed for Mother . . . two big windows that commanded the sea and the ships that sailed up and down . . . and little pleasure boats and the fishing fleet. It was any child's idea of heaven.

Mother sat down at the piano and she was not the least bit tired from the journey. Her fingers sought the keys and we heard the music again.

'Boys and girls come out to play
The moon doth shine as bright as day . . .'

I shall never forget what her music did to my heart. It stamped the night of Fergus's party deep into me for ever. The holiday was going to be a success. There was a wonderful excitement about settling into our quarters. We imagined we had never lived in such splendour with the sea just under our windows. The dining room was an acre of spotless table linen and there were chips with everything. Jackie said this was the 'vie en rose'. Marmee said she might prefer to have the evening meal upstairs and Rohan stayed with her. Downstairs, we behaved ourselves under the eye of Aunt Bessie and Annie and then Rohan took us out to see the town.

Mostly Mother had her meals sent up, because she liked it better that way. Sometimes, Rohan preferred it too, but often he took us out and it was a foreign world to us. There were evenings when we went on everything, the jollity farm, the roller coaster, the swing boats, the boating pool, the skating rink . . . the show on the pier . . .

It was very expensive and as the days went by, there seemed to be a feverishness of desperation about him, that Marmee could not join in the fun. Yet she seemed to be much better and content to watch. She did not want to try the helter-skelter, nor bingo, nor see the stalls where they wound the Seaport sugarstick, nor yet try the fish and chip booth. God help her! She tried to like it all for Rohan's sake, but he had made probably the one bad judgement in his life and he saw it too late. Yet she looked so well and happy with a high colour in her cheeks.

'I'll have dinner up again tonight. It's so peaceful, looking down on all the excitement. You take the children out and Bessie and Annie. You know you enjoy all the fun as much as they do.'

We would wander the pleasure miles and I sensed that he had small peace of mind. He must try to make it all come right. He would wonder along with the garish music stabbing the thoughts that would wander back to her in the hotel room.

'Soon I'll be home again,' she sighed. 'I'll have time to rest then. This is lovely for the children and they enjoy every moment of it.'

The Amusement Park was the best thing for all of us. The big dipper was Rohan's cyclone, to blow away all the thoughts that must have haunted him. I knew myself a coward for I hated it. Everytime I rode it, I got the idea in my head, at the very high spot, that the bolts that upheld us had no great solidity to them . . . no real craftsmanship, but what judge was I? The wood seemed ply and the rails were too fragile. The cars raced at full speed from the great height to which they had crawled . . . then a great plunging fall to a tunnel far off down below, that looked too narrow. The big wheel was bad enough but the roller coaster was a spider's web. You could see out across the sea from the top of it. Everybody was thrilled with it or so it seemed. The sky was torn with their screaming every time the cars swooped. There were boys from the fair that rode the coaster with a fine carelessness, in jeans and sweat shirts, day after day, bored with it all.

I could not rid myself of the way a car might snap its rails and go sailing out into the sky. There might be no need to pretend to scream then. I dared not tell the others I was afraid, but I was. That last night of the holiday, I went to the gypsy to have my fortune told and the holiday had seemed to rush to its end.

It was home tomorrow. This was our last night on the town.

'You're set on seeing the gypsy, Ann,' Rohan had said. 'It'll be a pack of lies, but if it's what you want, this is your last chance.'

So I had taken my last chance. Rohan had decreed that there was only time for one of us to visit the original Gypsy Lee and as I had been keen to see her, the lot fell on me. If everybody was to take turns, we would not be back to the hotel till midnight and he would be in the bankruptcy courts. I looked back at the small crowd gathered about the foot of the three steps to the caravan and I grinned at them and ignored their remarks, about dark handsome men and myself. Then I turned back into the spotless rather gloomy caravan and found the hard-faced chain-smoking gypsy. The caravan seemed full of gold china ornaments. For all the gold, it was gloomy. There was a table with a glass paperweight and the woman was brooding over it, a hen with a solitary egg. I had to sit down opposite her and she took my hands one after the other, accepted a ten-penny piece with no great enthusiasm.

'Is that all he give you?'

I nodded my head and she wanted my age and anything I could tell her.

I said that I came of a big family and she asked me if I thought she had no eyes in her head, but it was one reading for one fee. Then looking mighty bored about it, she started off.

'You're Irish by your tongue, so you're from across the sea. That's easy, but I'm not one to work like that.'

She lit a stick of incense and a cigarette at the same match. Maybe she turned a switch that got the crystal ball on the table glowing and milky and cloudy and swirling. She had a look in it and she seemed surprised. It was all part of her act,

or so I thought. She was making it up and I wanted nothing
to do with it any more, just to be out in the clean air again
and back with the others.

'You have a strange path to tread, lady. There's danger in
it but maybe you come out of it safe. Maybe you go too far,
for I see a fall, but that's not now. The danger's all about you
this minute, hitting out at you like a thunderstorm, but it lets
you go free with an empire gone out from under your
feet . . .'

She was engrossed in the crystal now, though she told me
it was 'going back on her'. She even gave it a shake.

'I think I have the whole of it and then it twists like a snake
and is gone. There's a thicket of people all about you to
shield you and there are paths, that you must choose . . . a
good future, if you pick the right way to go, but it's not easy.
I've never seen them so clearly in the glass, all these people.
There's a dark man, same as all you ladies pray for and he is
your king of hearts.'

She got out a grubby pack of cards and turned up the king
of hearts as proof and I said I had better be going . . . that
they were waiting for me outside the caravan.

'Aye, they're waiting on the ladder of time, but not for you.
They're all clear to me in that glass . . . never seen the like
before. The king of hearts is not there. He's away off. There
are so many people . . . an old lady with diamonds on her
fingers and she's maybe a tinker woman for all the pride
about her. She's a peasant woman surely for she lives with
peasants, God pity her! Unhappy I think, but I see you and
you lifting her up. Her ivory hands protect you, for you walk
in danger, but your king of hearts is beside you.'

The gypsy seemed exhausted with such a powerful fortune
as mine seemed to be. She poured a glass of gin into a
smeared tumbler, shot it down her throat and wiped the
sweat off her forehead. I thought that she had it in her head
to get more trade from Rohan. More than ever I wanted to
get away from her, but she had me by the wrist. Then after

another gaze into the glass ball, she went to the door and opened it and saw Rohan waiting at the foot of the steps.

'Did you sire them all, Master?' she said.

'Not quite,' he laughed at her. 'There're impatient to be off and I must go, for it's our last day. We're flying off home tomorrow.'

'Let me read your hand, sir. I can see yourself in the crystal.'

We got away but she came wheedling after us. He spun her another ten-penny piece and a second and she jumped after them as agile as a cat and still she would not let us free of her.

'Mind how you go, sir. Mind how your pretty ones go. Don't fly the sky for the space of three. There's no safety in the sky, so that only birds and fools can take to it and live . . .'

She was making a nuisance of herself, following us along to the caravans and getting angry, so that at last she threw back the silver coins at Rohan's feet.

'You people don't believe that the Romany can see what's to come, but there are those of us gifted. I'm not after coin, just to warn you. I saw it as clear as clear just now . . . and your treasure gone, master. Don't take to the skies to fly any more . . . keep your feet on the safe earth and make straight for their mother's nest . . .'

She seemed to disappear into the crowd and Rohan had not been impressed with her. Aunt Bessie picked up the silver that lay where he had given it to the gypsy and had his gift thrown back at him. Aunt Bessie was off to buy some rock to take home to Derrycreevy tomorrow and Rohan was arranging us in an orderly queue at the pay box of the roller coaster. He had collected Baby Alice into his arm and I was still impregnated with the sleazy atmosphere of the caravan. All of my fears of the roller coaster seemed to intensify. Quite suddenly, maybe I interpreted what the gypsy might have meant.

The cars were rolling up the first slope and I jumped down from the platform.

'I don't think we ought to go on this now, Father . . . not after what the gypsy said.'

'Run along with Aunt Bessie then. Your stomach's turned by the smell of the damned smoking incense.'

Aunt Bessie had gone and the children were all loaded on the switch-back railway. I stood back and watched their cars rise higher and higher.

'Come back! Come back!' I shouted out, but the wind carried my voice away. A policeman bent down to ask me what was wrong and I tried to tell him that I was afraid of what Rohan was doing. He was a kind man. He told me that he did not think much of the roller coaster himself, but it was as safe as houses. I was not to "frit" . . . He took me to a stall and bought me a bar of nougat. I stood below the roller coaster pay platform and I watched the first cars climb to the very high spot and pause on the brink, swing slowly into the taking off place and I knew what despair was. I looked up at Baby Alice on Rohan's shoulder, waving down to myself on the ground. Was there nothing I could do to convince them that a gypsy might have foreseen it? I went to the pay box window and asked a tough looking roustabout if I could get some people taken off the coaster.

'Not a chance, ducks! They'll be down in the twinkling of an eye. Just hang about a bit and the family will shoot out at the exit platform.' Then more impatiently, 'Get out of the road if you don't want to pay for a ride. We've no time to be assing up and down with the runs. What do you think we are? . . . don't make money that way. There's a girl like you over on the helter-skelter . . . went up last week with her little mat in her hand and she daresn't come down again. Reckon she'll be there till she does, or till Mother Goose flies away with her.'

I hid behind the pay box, for people were laughing at me. I was just another frightened child. I saw it all happen and I knew it was going to happen and I had tried my best and done nothing to stop the crash. In my head, it turned over and over, the familiar jingle.

'Ladybird, ladybird, fly away home.
Your house is on fire.
Your children are gone.
All except one and that's little Ann,
And she has crawled under the warming pan . . .'

It was all slotting into space, in a glass crystal of curds and whey in a gypsy caravan. The small cars of the switchback railway were sliding over the apex of the topmost point. They poised and then hurtled down. I saw Rohan spring out into space with Baby Alice in his arms. The rails were matchsticks, that snapped off into pieces of kindling. It was an impossible height for survival. The air was full of flying section of broken car and rails. Screams were tearing the darkening night and broken girders and sections of Meccano rails . . . thrown down, and splintered three-ply wood.

There were all the emergency lights ready to be snapped on, spotlights on the scene of loose sand that lay behind the hoardings . . . and shouting.

'The cars are in bits. Police and fire brigade urgently, and ambulances. For God's sake get some ambulances, quick . . . red disaster . . . I repeat . . . red disaster.'

I knelt in deep dune sand and the policeman was with me . . . the same man, with whom I had spoken.

He had a walkie-talkie in his hand.

'Get them down here quickly, all emergency services. It's a major accident. The front cars of the roller coaster are done for . . . I saw it happen myself.'

It was then that the numbness came. I maybe left my body and wandered out of my senses. It was not possible that the little pile of clothes in the deep dune sands were Rohan and the Zebedee twins and the others . . . all gone.

The dunes were littered with broken rails and flung piles of clothes and mounds covered with tarpaulin sheeting.

There were firemen and ambulance men. The ambulances were very white, backing up, creeping, in the white of arc lights. The elderly sergeant held me in the hollow of his arm. I was looking at Rohan with Baby Alice still held against his shoulder and her arms about his neck . . . and both of them dead. My own voice was steady enough as I made the identification . . . gave the home address. Home was another universe. Then somewhere, were the red-headed twins, asleep, so innocent, all mischief gone, pitiful. Meg was dead too. I do not know how I knew, only that in death she was very small, like a favourite doll. I heard my voice making the identities clear and the voice of the old sergeant, praising me for being a great girl.

I even told them about Aunt Bessie, who had gone to buy rock to take home and telling them about the hotel we were staying at. The old sergeant never left me and soon he collected a lady policeman. He smiled when I called the girl that. 'Police-woman'. He said 'Police lady perhaps. You've been a great help to us. Now let us help you a little . . .'

It was all a dream and I must soon wake up, I knew it, but the dream went on and on.

'My mother is at the Seaport Hotel. Maybe I just dreamt it, but I think it did happen.'

They were in contact with Ballyboy and the Dean. I sat it all out in the Police Station and they were very kind to me. They took me to the hotel and Marmee was there and Aunt Bessie. Soon I might wake up or so I thought . . . find myself at home in Derrycreevy in the big kitchen with Sarah and Dinny.

I went to bed with Marmee, close against her breast, and I dreamt it all again and woke up again. It seemed impossible that what had happened, had happened, and there was no turning back time. Rohan was lost to us. Holy God! They were all lost to us. My mind cut out this part of my life. There was no keeping it in. There was so much to do and nobody to do it, now Rohan was dead. I moved from one moment to the next and no reality in any bit of it. Here was a thing they called the Inquest and it was "an act of God" verdict with no negligence. I had no hint that it made Mother and Aunt Bessie and myself what might be called 'the new poor'. The Switch Back Railway owed us nothing. It was an accident. The Switch Back Railway had been serviced adequately. Anybody using it did so at their own risk. There was no evidence of failure on behalf of the fair ground people Holiday makers took risks . . .

The Dean flew over to Seaport and collected us. He even attended the inquest with me, for it was not fitting that Mother should go. It all moved so very slowly. There was the crematorium and the Dean still with me and no more reality to the Cremation than a puppet show might have had . . . I slammed my mind shut when somebody explained that we would 'take their ashes safe home' and knew that there was nothing but a bad dream to it all. I yearned for Derrycreevy. Derrycreevy came at last and it had no comfort for any of us. It was still an impossible nightmare, that would not let us wake up and live again. The whole thing tangled in my brain.

I kept saying it to Mother, but maybe I adopted Fergus's name for her.

'You have me, Marmee. We'll look after Rohan's Kingdom and I'll never leave you. I promise. I'll never leave you.'

I could not really believe that Rohan had gone for ever. We had been flown home by Aer Lingus and the Dean had taken us to Derrycreevy in his car. I thought that the terror might be better at home but it was no different. The gold letters were painted on the black of the gate. It was time for me to wake up. Here I must find myself safe and know that it had all been a nightmare. Sarah was alive and Dinny and Michael. I tried to work out that Annie had stayed with Mother that night and she was safe home with us now. There was such a realisation coming up in front of me that I could never understand. I must go to sleep, but there was no sleep. Mama Cluny came to see us, all tears. Quite suddenly, I remembered the Zebedee twins, both dead. It was awful. She was dazed as we seemed to be. A doctor called and gave her an injection . . . took her home to Gorse Hill House in his car, left her some blue capsules to take, put a hand on my black hair and told me he was very sorry about the tragedy.

Mostly the Dean seemed to be in Derrycreevy and I sat in on strange discussions. Sometimes, I hardly understood what people were talking about. The ashes were coming home by plane. Desmond McCarthy, our solicitor, would receive them. The interment was strictly private. I was excluded from this. Later I knew that Fergus Cluny and Aunt Bessie and the Dean and Dinny and Michael and the Vicar were alone on the side of the Cemetery Hill. I wondered why Aunt Bessie was so silent that day and why Fergus came to visit me. It was all over. There was to be something called a combined Memorial Service, but not yet. Just for now, a house that was impossibly deserted . . . no sound, no laughter . . . just an emptiness. It was a time in my life when I could not get rid of the confusion that possessed me. It was my duty to snap out of it. Dinny was all muddled up and was calling me 'Miss Baby' again. Any more than any of us could believe it, he could not accept it that Rohan was dead. The days passed slowly and then it was upon us, the Memorial Service. Derrycreevy was full of people . . . Mother's family from Cloncon, some of the Rowan aunts from Screebogue, patients in their Sunday clothes, the dignitaries of Ballyboy, the representative of so many different things, the Police, the British Legion, the Clergy, the Navy . . . people and things, that I could not recognise. The church was going to be crowded, but first it was the House itself. I moved like a marionette on strings and seemed to be able to talk. I was quite free of myself in the black dress, able to understand what I must say.

It was any old-fashioned funeral or memorial service in

Ireland, even in this day and age. The people came so respectfully and talked to us and maybe made orations over the dead . . . small unsophisticated words of memories that had been. There was to be a reception after the church for drinks and food. I seemed to remember the preparations for it the night before, with us all in the kitchen . . . and the glasses all laid out in the hall and the buffet in the dining room and the furniture polished and the silver gleaming . . .

The church was packed to overflowing. The town might have been dead for the way the shops were all closed and houses had their blinds drawn. The people stood in the street as we went past and the men's caps off . . . and each person made the sign of the cross as the line of cars passed. They stood by as we went into the church and we were to sit in the front pews . . . the families. I watched myself go up along the aisle and hoped that Mother would not die with sorrow. She was so white, that she looked dead. I gathered her hand into mine and found myself in the front row in the seat next the aisle and that was Rohan's seat. I must shut my senses to everything that was said, I decided, and then Fergus came in, pushed his way into Rohan's place and knelt to pray. After a while he sat up, hurt my hand with the grasp of it.

'You'll be all right now,' he whispered against my ear, 'the sailor is home from sea.'

It was a pity that they chose such heart-breaking music. As a background somebody had picked 'Morning has broken like the first morning . . . Blackbirds are singing before break of day . . .'

The superb song possessed every corner of the church and soared to the vaulted ceiling and possessed us beyond our escape . . . Yet after a while, in my heart, there was a descant to it. I heard the music-box tune.

'Boys and girls come out to play . . . the moon doth shine as bright as day'. Maybe it was I, who drew them back. The thought terrifies me, even now. Maybe I succeeded too, to bring the ghosts back to the moonlight nights.

Then we were out in the open air and mixed up in a confusion of waiting cars. Mother went home with Aunt Bessie. Fergus shoved me into his car and we were away.

'Ladybird,' he said. 'From now on, it will get better. I'll be near enough to watch out for my house and Rohan's. Matthew Langdon calls you "Lady Bird". He told me you have a warming pan like Ann in the Fly-Away-Home nursery rhyme. He told me last night that you have enough laughter left in you to slam the gates of hell . . . and my God, it's been hell . . .'

The reception at the house was over at last and everybody was gone. Then I came back to the hall and stood on the Celtic carpet and put my hand on the banisters and knew that never again . . . Then I really knew the emptiness of it all. There was void and nullity and I was so tired that I thought I might die of it. That was the first night I dreamt that I was back at Fergus's Coming-of-Age party.

I heard the singing under my window and was too sleepy to wake up from the dream.

'Boys and girls come out to play,
The moon doth shine as bright as day . . .'

I got up and went to the window after a time and wondered if they still lingered, but the moonlit lawns were empty, only for mistiness like fine gauze. Then for a fraction of time I saw them . . . in the tableau of children in old-fashioned ivory satin dress . . . crinolines, knee breeches, silk top hats, hands joined to dance in a circle. There was happiness all about them. Just a split fraction of time and an upsurge of clear voices in song . . . Then the lawns were empty and the song was gone and Derrycreevy was deserted and I saw that maybe I was shut out for eternity in loneliness . . .

Yet there was no doubting that they had been there and had gone again. The clouds were sweeping along to blot out the full moon and the wind was rising, but I had surely seen the children. I knew that there had been a whisper in

Ballyboy that the house was haunted, but Ballyboy was a place that could produce haunted houses with little excuse for it. I was mazed with sleep. I went back to bed and knew what loneliness was. It was gone for ever, the happiness. Never again would Rohan come home and call from the hall.

'Hear this! Hear this! Rohan is home.'

He had not been with them tonight and I ached to see him again. He must be somewhere about. I could sense him. Then I thought I heard the voice I loved. No, I did hear it – soft and clear.

'Don't fret, Ann Catherine. Rest tranquil and it will all flow past you. Just try to hold on to Derrycreevy. It will come back again for I can see it, all youth and laughter again . . . and mind my sheep. God! Mind my sheep for me . . . Marmee and Dinny and Michael and Annie and Sarah . . . and the sick ones. It's a lot I ask of you, but I know you can do it. Mind my sheep . . . if you do nothing else – for the love we have one for the other –Ann Catherine.'

I knew what it was to cry all night in the loneliness of Derrycreevy and Rohan and all his pretty chickens gone for aye.

CHAPTER TWO

'Boys and girls come out to play'

That was what had happened on the night of the Memorial
Service. I was overtired and overwrought. I had a vivid
imagination. I tried to settle down and count my blesssings.
I had Mother and Aunt Bessie. Aunt Bessie seemed to have
achieved a new image. She had become a person of great
courage and strength. Sarah and Annie had taken on the
housekeeping. Dinny and Michael had seen to the outside
work. The car was always washed and waiting, in case it was
wanted. Vegetables appeared automatically from the
garden. The whole place was just as it had always been,
although it was impossible that this could be so. There were
no surgeries or visits or mysterious calls in the night. Maybe
the house was dead . . . killed with silence. Emergency Ward
Ten had been turned off at the switch of the Box. The
excitement was lost . . . nothing to be done but the messages
in town. I went along on my bike because petrol cost money.

It was time that Rohan's affairs were settled. There was a
will to be read, but no hurry to the reading of it. Desmond
McCarthy warned me that it was not good. Desmond's
father had looked after the house in Rohan's father's time . . .
and so on back for generations. Well I knew the deed boxes
in Desmond's offices, with ROHAN painted on the red sides
and a deal of dust overall and a window that looked out on a
narrow garden, completely neglected.

So the will was to be read and Annie and Sarah expected
to put on dinner in the dining room and then the cloth drawn

and the red sealing-wax broken down across the mahogany and all the benefactors gathered round the table. Desmond released us from a deal of formality. He arrived in one day with the will bound in red tape and sealed . . . accepted a pint of beer in the kitchen and sat himself on a corner of the table there. Maybe Annie and Sarah thought we were done out of the grandeur of it, but there was no grandeur left any more. The whisper was creeping about Ballyboy and it was frightening us all. I had tried to say thanks to them, but I knew that if I gave them the Keys of the Kingdom, I'd have fallen short. Maybe there was nothing to give.

At any rate, Desmond cut all ceremony. He broke the seal and read out that this was the last will and testament of Dr. John Rohan of Derrycreevy House in the town of Ballyboy . . . and then he caught sight of my face and shot off short, just folded the parchment and pushed it into his side pocket.

'It's a typical will,' he said. 'I wasn't able to get him to be formal about it. I'll tell you it's not good, but I know that John Rohan would like me to say at once that he owes much to "the faithful people, who served him" and that's all of you here . . . Annie and Sarah, Dinny and Michael, that what he has left you is only a token of his love for you and his gratitude . . . Miss Hamilton too, Aunt Bessie of course, for she was one of the foundations of the happiness of his family.'

They were in no way disappointed that the sum was only fifty pounds each. It might have been a fortune. Dinny was to have his gold watch, because of the watch Dinny kept on his front door all the years. Michael was to have the gold medal, that Rohan had won in medicine, because Michael had conquered tuberculosis and *that* was a victory worth while.

Desmond looked at Mother and smiled, said softly that Rohan would like her to provide a home in Derrycreevy House for Annie and Sarah and Dinny and Michael, no matter what happened, if it was possible to do.

'He said to me, Mrs. Rohan, that you might need fighters

when he was gone and he hoped it would not be so, but if it was so, "Maybe I've left her the fighters to look after her. I don't know." '

There were so many small bequests . . . his chess board to Dean Matthew Langdon, a Chippendale carver's Chair to Mrs. Constance Hamilton of Cloncon . . . to Aunt Bessie, his bay mare with black points, the governess car and the harness thereof, because there had been a time when Aunt Bessie's life had been happy with horses, so he would leave her some joy.

Desmond smiled across at Aunt Bessie.

'He had a great affection for you, Miss Hamilton. He said that you had been through the crash of a great empire, and he'd never see you without a horse to drive, while he had possessed such a thing himself to give. He laughed a lot about the will . . . never thought to die so soon. It was a light-hearted affair. I remember that day well. He said that you'd learned to laugh in the face of hell, Miss Hamilton . . . learned it from our good Dean Langdon. You all know how the Dean lectured us about the properties of laughter.'

I remember thinking that the will did not seem solemn, but Desmond had been steeling himself for the end and here it came . . . 'I warned you. John Rohan did not know the sands were low in his hour-glass . . . well nigh run out. He was never a man to keep his accounts straight, send his bills out regularly . . . see to insurance and prepare for the future. He was so busy living, that he never thought of dying.'

Desmond stopped here and for a long time. We had started to think that was the end of it, when he went on.

'The residue of the estate goes to his wife and after that to be divided equally between his children . . .'

There was another silence and Desmond was avoiding looking at any of us. Then at last he went on.

'It leaves but one child now . . . Ann Catherine. It will all end with Ann.'

I had not realised the final picture, but he went on with it and his teeth worried his lower lip and he could not look at Mother nor yet at me.

'The final estate is small. You must prepare yourselves, every one of you. The future of this house is black. You must get ready for change . . . total change . . . I'm sorry, more sorry than I could ever say.' He had left it a long time to get over the first shock of death. He was a kind man, Desmond.

So a will had been a joke to Rohan, who had never foreseen the roller coaster, had never probably accepted the fact of Mother with a coronary clot. It was certain that we must now sell Derrycreevy to the highest bidder. It was all very well for Mother and me to look at each other and to vow silently that never would we part from Derrycreevy. Desmond looked sadder than ever.

'There's a grapevine in Ballyboy. You've heard it no doubt, every one of you. "They" say that this house is haunted now. "They" have it that the children in ivory satin still dance the lawns and sing the tune from the music box. There are those, that say they've come to fetch Miss Ann away, but I'd advise you not to believe that. A haunted house in Ireland has no sales value. We're stuck with Derrycreevy now for a while at least. Maybe it suits us, for none of you want to sell it. I very much fear the fine house will end up with the rats and the jackdaws.'

My whisper echoed up into the corners of the kitchen ceiling.

'It's true, it's haunted. One night, I heard them singing and I looked out. I wanted to go to them, but they were away and I wanted them back. They were real and they were happy . . . so happy . . .'

'If you tell us this now, Ann, you cut the throat of Derrycreevy House.'

'But it's true. I saw them. They were there and the music just the same and if I had had courage to go down to them, I'd be with them now.'

'That's it then,' Desmond said. 'So what do we do now? You'll get no bidder for the house, for who will go against God or maybe the devil?'

'We don't want to sell Derrycreevy,' Mother said. 'Let's wait a wee while. There's furniture and fine furniture too. We can sell it. We could sell some of the garden stuff . . . maybe eggs and home-made jams and jellies, sort of stuff we used to give for sale at the church fêtes . . . cakes and that. We'd get by.'

Desmond's elbows were on the kitchen table and his head in his hands, but Dinny still could not stop looking at the gold watch and the chain. I went to him and helped him with the winding of it and showed him how it went in his waistcoat pocket and the chain through the right button-hole and still he never ceased to admire it and asked if anybody wanted the time.

Desmond's voice cut across the business in the kitchen, and it was despair made him do it.

'And rates and taxes and food and repairs and wages?' he asked in a sharp voice, as if he was angry at us suddenly. 'Is it charity you want, Mrs. Rohan, from such a proud house?'

'We'll scrape along for a while anyway, Desmond,' Aunt Bessie said. 'We have produce from the garden and Dinny will see to that. We could get the hens to produce more. We might even keep a little Kerry cow and sell milk and butter. We'd all work at it.'

'Miss Baby will save us all,' cried Dinny. 'Didn't she save me when I came home from the wars, for it was the Lord God sent her looking for me and she put out her little arms and claimed me as her own, promised me that I'd not have to wander the earth.'

Oh! God. I was deputed to be 'Miss Baby' once more and the tears almost burst their bonds, but Fergus had arrived late for the appointment, and quite suddenly he was there, somewhere along the morning and nothing decided, he was there. Desmond had summoned him to the reading of the will for Rohan had left him some Captain's decanters and an Admiral Fitzroy barometer – and the wish that his seas might remain calm. Fergus was very sympathetic, when he saw the state that had arisen in the household . . . said that he would be very grateful, if he might let the bequests to him lie where they had always been, and that did not mean that he was ungrateful, only that such things should never leave Derrycreevy.

'There's nothing left only the furniture and Miss Ann is being difficult about the rocking horse,' said Annie. 'What can a wood horse feel?'

Fergus put his arm round Annie and told her that she might be surprised. Maybe the rocking horse was a pookah that could take her on his back and fly away with her, if she was ten years old again. It was strange the magnetism he seemed to have, Fergus Cluny. It seemed to me that he solved the near future in a few minutes. Mother had been taken off to bed by Aunt Bessie and it was all over. It was clear to me that she had given up the idea of struggling against fate any more.

Desmond asked me if I had any idea of what it cost to run the estate, even for one week.

'We'd not *want* wages,' they all said.

'And the rates then and the taxes, if you're to live on blackberries and mushrooms?' he pressed me.

'Let's try it, McCarthy.' said Fergus quietly. 'At least you can strike school fees off the expenses. In view of the tragedy, the schools have waived their fees. Doubtless you knew it. The Dean just met me and he told me . . . don't know how he knew. I wonder if the schools realise the joy the children would have had in not having to go back this term?'

'So I can stay in Derrycreevy for ever?' I said and that decided it. I'd stay here for ever and never go away to school again and it would all come right. I don't know how I knew it, but it would work out, one day.

Fergus had put his arm about my shoulders.

'No more boarding school, but Matthew Langdon is determined to see that you get schooling and he's a man of his word. I don't think he'll want you far away from Ballyboy for a year or two. Just do the best you can. Stay put here.'

Desmond gave good lawyer's advice now, to a fourteen-year-old child, and all the house retainers listening. He sounded in despair.

'I can't advise it. It won't work,' he said. 'You'll become a charge on the parish, if that's what you want. I've explained it. Sell your furniture bit by bit . . . and a dozen eggs and vegetables. When did anybody ever have to pay for the stuff they were given from Derrycreevy? Buy pigs and try to sell pork. What do you know of it? It's probably not legal. Open your eyes, Ann, and accept a lost cause.'

'Just a few months Desmond,' I pleaded and Fergus echoed for me . . . 'Just a few months. Don't break her heart. We might do the impossible. Marmee will be able to stay in her home.'

'And the new doctor gives Mrs. Rohan no more than two years,' Desmond said. 'Ann knows it. It's all hers, this insoluble problem. Ann will become the sole residual legatee.'

'Shut up, Desmond.' Fergus said sharply and I was horrified to think that mine was the total responsibility or soon would be Always I had gone to Mother to ask what to do, but presently she might have happily gone to Rohan, and I would have no judge but myself and – I was only a child with a child's sense.

'I thought we could buy geese for the Christmas trade. We could fatten pigs. A Kerry cow would be easy to manage. We might make things as we did for the church fêtes, but sell them and use the money. We'd got to make money. Rohan said in his will that we must look after our people, not have them homeless. 'I'll find out how to make money, if it's the last thing I do.' I whispered to myself. 'There are hazel nuts and sloes and crab-apples. We'll start a market with the shops.'

So blackberries became food to sell . . . mushrooms and elderberries and hazel nuts. Ballyboy knew the straits we were in. Marmee must not be worried with it. They dealt with me kindly and maybe they remembered Rohan's humanity. The year dragged by and Fergus had gone back to hospital again, but I remembered the manliness of his chest against the softness of my breast and the Rohan-man smell of him and the look in his eyes, of pity and maybe a little love.

So we persisted in trying to survive. There seemed little change in Mother, but the quarter days dragged by. She was just any old soldier, who was fading quietly away. I knew it, but there was nothing I could do. I was very glad of the Dean and my homework. Yet there were happy days, I knew, when we drove out in the governess cart with the bay mare. I think that Mother had tempted Aunt Bessie back to live in the past. I thought of her as Mother, but always "Marmee" crept in. Fergus's name for her.

Michael would have the mare harnessed and ready. At half past two, we would trot smartly out through the gates of Derrycreevy House and straight into the high-days of Glen Leven. I said nothing. I went along with them and listened.

Maybe I had crab apples to pick, or hazel nuts . . . maybe a sloe tree to strip for sloe wine.

They had been daughters of Glen Leven estate, daughters of Angus Hamilton, my grandfather. Grandmother had been the heiress of another great estate . . . Strawberry Hill. Of course, I knew it all. It had become our legend, but I could never hear it often enough. Grandmother 'had so many children that she did not know what to do.' Hamilton's Glen Leven was such a demesne that 'ran three miles along the road'. There had been great stables and every child had his or her own steed and they all rode to hounds. The entertaining was fabulous with dinners and balls and no expense spared. It was a super story. We had always been thrilled with it. Grandfather Hamilton had been a kind of prodigal son. He had wasted his money and then he had been killed in a hunting accident. He had broken his neck over a double bank and had been carried home dead on a hurdle.

He had left them all penniless and homeless like the mice in Rabbie Burns' nest, run down by the coulter. Angus Hamilton had left sorrow after him. Glen Leven had to go. The family had to make what homes they could. It was all very sad and a great story or so we had always thought. Of course, we knew Grandmother, whom we called the "Heiress of Strawberry Hill". When the crash came, she had moved into the Hunt Cottage, called Cloncon, and that meant "the Meadow of the Hounds" in Gaelic It was a very poor place after Glen Leven, but it was one of the Glen Leven "tied farms". With her, she had taken Uncle James and Aunt Kate and maybe Aunt Bessie, but the rest of the children "had been scattered across the face of the earth".

I had picked the story up bit by bit. We were all afraid of the Heiress of Strawberry Hill in the good old days of Derrycreevy. When we visited at the Meadow of the Hounds, she never seemed to have much opinion of us.

Aunt Bessie had been the eldest child and Marmee the baby. The cause of the smash was drink and prodigality . . . that and a toss out hunting at the double bank. On the drives now, I picked more details.

If the mistress wanted a white mare for her birthday, Hamilton would ride a pure-bred Arab up the front steps of Glen Leven . . .

It was the stuff romances are made of. I remember the afternoons in the governess cart and the loveliness of the hedges and the roses blooming still and ripe blackberries for jelly, that must go to the shops now against the cost of tea and sugar. Maybe I learned all about the past during those drives, but perhaps I did not.

'The Heiress of Strawberry Hill was the catch of the whole county,' Mother told me proudly. 'Your grandfather was a gentleman, of course, with a fine estate, but she could have had any of the fine gentlemen. Her father never did approve of him and there was a great unhappiness when she married him.'

Aunt Bessie had smiled at me across the governess cart one day.

'It seems to me that you and I, Ann, have had the experience of finding ourselves "penniless lasses wi' a lang pedigree". In the days of the crash of Glen Leven, I recall the scatter of the rats in front of the terriers at harvest threshing. Paw was dead, and Maw too proud to ask help from her father, so we set out to make bricks without straw and a sorry job it was. Poor Paw had tried to see that ,I had a good education. The eldest daughter is always her father's joy and pride and I was to go to Cambridge University to Girton. Then there was no money. Same thing's familiar to you, Honey. I thought life had gone out from beneath me, like the rotten floor of a barn. Looking back, I can see the way your aunts and uncles scattered. I went out as a companion-housekeeper. Then Rohan came one day and rescued me and took me home to Derrycreevy, after he married your mother. Derrycreevy is such a happy house, full of the miserable people that Rohan picked up on his travels. I always think that this patch of earth on the side of a river was marked out for a sanctuary. Even with Rohan gone, there's magic here. Nobody is ever turned away.'

It cheered us up to turn time back. "Maw and Paw", Aunt Bessie and Mother called their parents, and I listened to their talk about all that had gone on and picked a wild harvest. If the brambles scratched my skin, I thought of the rows of jars we would have soon . . . bramble jelly . . . hazel nut by the pound to be picked. "Derrycreevy Produce" we called it and later it would be traded to the shops against the things we had to buy. I would think of the credits – the milk of the small Kerry cow and the butter. The hens gave us eggs and the geese were for the Christmas trade. Yet I knew the struggle it was to break even. I felt sorry when the season came to watch the spawning salmon face the weir.

Then a day I remember, when "Maw" called on a visit to us, took me by the shoulders and cried 'Nil desperandum'. I had thought her a strange old lady – all contradictions – diamonds on her ivory fingers, yet a white grubby shawl – a green glass brooch in her cravat – the look of a Royal queen – maybe the Czarina of all the Russians – and me by the shoulders and 'Do not despair'. I had loved her peasant's cottage as a little child, for all the way it was a crofter's dwelling. Here was Maw, my grandmother, the Czarina – the Heiress of Strawberry Hill – landed gentry once upon a time.

'Rohan was another like my husband,' she said. 'I don't think your mother knew what breeding was. Some men are caught up with breeding. I wonder if your mother wanted so many children, but she was so very much in love. She's had that at least.'

She looked down at me.

'You're a good girl, Ann. There's no stopping you. Books and husbandry and you're making a fight for it. I wasn't one to fight, after I ended in Cloncon. Oh, Ann! I know how it feels – the decline and fall, but don't blame yourself for what was an act of God. They tell me that Dean Langdon had you worked past bearing with your studies, but do your best for him. You're the one filly foal left from all this old house and the sire gone for ever and your mother's heart is breaking for Rohan. You see if I'm not right. She'll not live without him.'

This was a thought that filled me with terror. I knew I must never let Rohan's house go, but the quarter days had been adding up two years and I was almost sixteen then sixteen past and there was no progress only for the worse in Mother's health.

The house was becoming a patchwork place, try as we

might. There was no doubt now, that it was haunted. It was as if the "Boys and Girls" refused to desert it. Sometimes, I would go into the nursery and find the rocking horse still moving gently and the stirrups swinging. Often there was the quiet whisper in a corner . . . and once the mad rushing of feet along the landing to the banisters and then laughter in the hall below. Always I ran to find what it was, and found nothing, but at night sometimes, I saw them dance in the garden just the same and knew they were there and Rohan with them, so knew them luckier than I.

I was sixteen the day Fergus came home again. I was beginning to realise that I was getting nowhere. I was beginning to know that Mother was almost lost and with her would go all we had fought for.

He came down the hill to the river, jumping like a mountain goat, and found me fishing for salmon in the shallow water down from the weir. I climbed out of the river and ran to him and perhaps I was so pleased to see him that I forgot propriety. I saw his arms open to me and I ran to him and was enclosed in safety again. It was a long time since I had known safety. I buried myself in it and hid my face in his shoulder, so that he could not see my tears.

'If I'd known you were coming . . .'

It must have been a long time till we brought ourselves up to date with news. Then he started in to put my affairs to rights in the Fergus manner.

'You won't accept our help, Mother says, but you'll have to see sense. The haunting has put paid to the selling of the house and Marmee will never see the place go, and you're mule-stubborn about keeping it for Rohan . . . but darling Ann, the new doctor has established himself. He's got a small modern lay-out and he's a good chap. You'll have to let Derrycreevy go. I know it's a place for Annie and Sarah and Michael and Dinny. Mother tries to help you best she can, but she worries that a crash is coming. You'll have to face it. It's time you really opened your eyes.'

He knew it all and so he told me. He knew that the Dean came to the house as often as he had always done and gave me homework that made my head ache. He knew that Aunt Bessie helped me with it and often we worked till midnight. This was my education. He knew we were up at dawn for "the husbandry" of the little "farm". He had only to look at me to see I was shabby. The years had crawled too slowly and I had watched the battle being lost. Maybe Fergus knew that the doctor had told me that Marmee would not last the year.

Fergus and I were sitting on the seat under the big chestnut tree on the river bank.

'I'm on leave from the hospital now, Ann, but I won't be able to get away freely any more, and I'm committed to the Navy . . . deeply committed. There are no Gorse Hill sons left . . . no Zebedee twins. I'll not be free to come and go, as I would like to. The Clunys always owe a son . . . tradition, and I'm "it" now. I can't leave you on your own with what will happen. I've talked to Desmond about it. I know you well by now and I know when you make up your mind and set on a thing, there you stick. I thought of an idea that might work and Desmond thought it was the best of a bad bargain. Just let him tell you and bear with us if you can. It might work . . . see me to the top of the hill, Ann.'

At the top, we looked down on Ballyboy and then he said he would be over in the morning, and I had perforce to ask him to supper for I had caught a salmon. That evening, we ate a very fine fish and pretended to be very merry about it. Marmee, Aunt Bessie and Fergus and myself . . . and there seemed no cloud in the sky, yet I knew that Desmond McCarthy was to see us the next day . . . than it was goodbye to Fergus, for he was back to base first thing in the morning . . . a recall.

Desmond and I sat on the same riverside seat under the chestnut the next morning and he was the stern young lawman and my heart was lonely for Fergus.

'We're not winning, Ann. The whole structure is going. You must give up the effort you're making, just because of a thing in your father's will. So you must keep Annie and Sarah and Dinny and Michael? Did he know what this would mean, Rohan, when he wrote it? You'll not survive, Ann, not in this day and age, but Fergus, knowing you, says you can do it. It seems he has great faith in you and so have I. I think it might work, God damn me, if I don't!'

'Tell me Desmond, and don't lie to me.'

'You realise that your mother is dying and you want her to die as she has lived in Derrycreevy and the mercy dust thrown in her eyes. You want to take her out in the trap and talk about the old days with Aunt Bessie and maybe you both know just what you're trying to do.'

I nodded my head.

'Let her go then in peace . . . just wait that long. Then close the place up. Now I've as near as damn fixed it. I've got a roof for your head in "the meadow of the hounds". That's disposed of, God help you! Then the Dean can fix Sarah and Annie in the Convent for a while and Michael and Dinny will move into the stable premises, as outdoor caretakers. That will make the rates on Derrycreevy nil, for it's not occupied. We put dust sheets over the furniture and let Derrycreevy sleep. Christ, Ann! The Doctor gives your mother no time at all . . . but we wait.'

I knew the slough of despair then. There were so many people wanting to help me.

'I will never accept charity,' I muttered.

I was ashamed for the kindness of Ballyboy . . . the gifts left on our doorstep anonymous, the warm kindness from this one small town, the fresh doughnuts straight from the boiling fat in Oakley's bakehouse . . . the sliced home-cooked ham from old Oakley's carving fork and me doing the shopping . . . the fresh baked cake from this one or that one, the bunch of flowers, the hundredweight of potatoes – all gifts.

'Now listen and listen properly, you proud person,' Desmond said. 'Close the whole house. The Dean has promised me that the Convent will take Annie and Sarah and be glad of them, just for a year or two. Michael and Dinny will be quite able to look after the stable cottage and themselves and keep an eye on the house. You know well that Mrs. Cluny would put you up in Gorse Hill as long as you like to stay . . .'

'I will never accept charity,' I said. 'Mrs. Cluny is like myself – the new poor. She just scrapes by . . .'

'Christ, Ann! The furniture is going bit by bit. Let's put it in dustsheets and close the place up, before it's all gone. Let Derrycreevy sleep. Please, Ann. Please . . . but only after Marmee is gone . . . to Rohan.'

I nodded my head and repeated after him. 'So be it then, but only when . . . when . . .'

'Empty, there'll be no rates nor yet taxes. We'll get by, Ann. God knows how you'll fare at Cloncon, but it will all be legal . . . or I think it will . . . Bless you. You're a lovely woman grown. Only the other day, you were a scrubby boy. Did I tell you the Czarina of all the Russias wants you as guest at Cloncon – and your Aunt too.'

'Fergus told me,' I said.

I went to bed that night and slept the sleep of the dead. I had prayed as I never prayed before.

'Please don't let her die, God . . . only if she can't live without Rohan. If that's the way of it, take her but gently, take her. Thy will be done . . .'

Yet never would I give up Derrycreevy and the happy place it had once been. The music box tinkled in the background of my dreams.

> 'Boys and girls come out to play
> The moon doth shine as bright as day.
> Leave your supper and leave your sleep
> Join your playfellows in the street . . .'

They were on the lawn and the moon riding high in the

sky. Here were the people I had seen as little mounds in the deep dunes and tarpaulins flung over them, or maybe, later on, sleeping in the mortuary, and grown small, like poor Meg.

There was a celestial descant, that filled the whole sky and there was a light, far more brilliant than the night of Fergus's party. It would have dimmed the Chinese lanterns, to ha'penny candles.

They were on the lawn below my window, hands joined and dancing in a circle, beckoning me to come to them. I saw Jackie smile at me and the Zebedee twins and Baby Alice, doing her best to keep her feet in the dancing circle. Rohan himself held aloof, as if he wondered at the wisdom of what they planned and about him the echo of his voice . . . 'Hear this! Hear this! Where are my pretty chickens?'

I slid my window open, as they beckoned to me, leaned out over the sill. It was a big drop to the stone verandah, but I had only to take one step for peace. It only wanted the courage.

Some more of the furniture must go, I must not disappoint them. Yet it was then, I saw her clearly, come walking through the glass of the french window below me. She was dressed in gauze light, Marmee, and the glass did not halt her. She reached the stones of the verandah, and they all came running to her and she had Baby Alice in her arms and Rohan turning to watch her. Rohan had come home. It was the oldest memory of them all . . . and I was left behind. The children were gathered round Rohan just as they had always done and I shrank back from the brightness of the light. Then I ran too, but not to the window and across the sill to join with them. I went towards the door, my mind half understanding what had happened. I closed the window and slashed the curtains shut. The floor was cold to my feet. I was down the stairs and along to Mother's room on the flight below my bedroom. I let them go. I opened the door to her room and saw she was sleeping. My bare feet felt the softness of the carpet and at the bedside, the white sheepskin rug. She slept, but she had gone and my head was on her bosom. I knew complete stillness and maybe complete happiness. It was finished.

'Don't fret, honey,' she said to me across time and I knew that it was true that there was a life beyond death. It was no tragedy, no pain, only a great faith. I tucked the bedclothes round her and let her sleep. It would be time enough to open the house to sorrow again at the dawning of the new day, yet I knew that Derrycreevy was mine now and that Derrycreevy was still a fortress for the holding, as Rohan had decreed, and the task was mine and mine alone, for if I did not do as Desmond had instructed me, then Derrycreevy would be broken at last.

Mother must be laid to rest.

I moved on to another plane of life. I was sixteen. Fergus had gone away or else I might not have felt so lost. He was a naval doctor, aged 23, and perhaps by now he thought he had got my affairs settled and had forgotten all about me.

I try to put the funeral out of my mind, but it will not be put out. The church had been full and Derrycreevy had been full. They were all gathered there, all the household of the big house and a cohort from Cloncon, and strangers that I did not even know. Desmond had summoned us for the reading of the will, sitting at the head of the dining room table this time and the red blood of the seal rattling down on the polished mahogany.

I was the sole residual legatee this time and the future of the house was up for a decision. They had all come into the room, the Dean and Aunt Bessie and Dinny and Michael and my grandmother of Cloncon. Uncle James had been there and had taken himself off, taken Dinny and Michael off with him to the kitchen, to talk about ferrets. There was an Alice in Wonderland air to it. Cloncon folk had come in a clapped-out car with a woolly dog that belonged to Maw. 'Might the devil fly away with him,' said Uncle James.

Everytime the door between the passage to the kitchen from the dining room opened, Uncle James's voice echoed through to our ears . . .

'Do ye two know how to work a ferret? Do ye have the know-how to set a gin-trap? I'm a great man for the ferreting myself and I've an animal called Tiger in my pocket this minute . . . gentle as a dove. I'll show ye what's to do . . . nothing to it.'

It was an informal meeting in the dining-room and it had all been settled without me. Mrs. Constance Hamilton was the important guest, for she was to take me into custody and nobody could stand in her way. She had the small white poodle on a silk square handkerchief and he seemed to want to join the ferreting enthusiasts in the kitchen. Every time Uncle James's voice was heard from the kitchen, the old lady, his mother, stiffened with disapproval.

'Great lubberly boy!' she said. 'My eldest son and not fit to be produced in the dining-room. There's your Uncle James, Ann, fathered by Hamilton of Glen Leven on me. I'll never understand it.'

'There are some pieces of furniture I'll not part with,' I whispered. 'Nothing from the nursery or from our common room. They may want to come and play sometimes.'

'The girl is off her head,' said Maw, with a piercing look at me, but she went on as if I had said nothing.

'It's no good pretending to yourself, Ann. It can't be done without drastic measures. We call a halt now and change courses. We must do it. I'm taking you and my daughter, Bessie, home to Cloncon to live as my guests and a welcome to you. McCarthy here will see to the legal side of it. He's an honest boy . . .'

She went on as if she owned the world and the woolly dog sometimes stopped barking, so we heard something – not much. He had taken a desire to nip Desmond's ankles and he sallied forth from the silk square to the floor and back again for refuge. Desmond managed to land one secret kick at him and that intensified the war and I wondered if we were all going mad.

'Let's have the accounts out, McCarthy,' Maw said, and poor Desmond was apologetic to her for the mess we had made of it, he and I.

'Wages, rates and taxes? So much capital and so little left. So much for furniture sold and that was treachery . . . small change for pigs and eggs and geese. A few pence for pots of jam and home baked cakes, so we're in trade now and crab-apples and sloes and mushrooms for credit and not for fun any more,' said Maw.

The Dean had one of my hands in his and he told me gently that Sarah and Annie would be happy in the Convent and that the men would be happy in the stable cottage, would be able to look after themselves and to act as caretakers.

'It'll work out. You'll see it will!'

Maw's decision was final.

'My daughter, Bessie, and you, Ann, will drive the bay mare over to Cloncon tomorrow and you're welcome there as long as you wish to stay. My "Meadow of the Hounds" still and not one hound left of them all . . . Growler and Faithful and Bellman and True. All gone with the days. Let Derrycreevy sleep with Rohan. We'll beat the tax-man for the way they fell on Glen Leven like vultures. Ann Rohan must have a roof over her head, while we work out ways and means. It's not the first time I've sat in on a will, but the next will be my own, and the last – thanks be to God!'

She brooded almost to herself.

'Given time, I might have saved Glen Leven, but Hamilton was dead. Given time and a brave heart, I'd have done it, but I hadn't the courage left. I think, Ann, that you have the heart of a lioness. Bessie was a good girl too. Bessie and James said we should shut up Glen Leven and I laughed it to scorn. I'm sorry for it now. I wanted done with it, so Bessie she ran away to be a companion to some vinegary old lady. James was like a brigand. He'd have had us all hanged, for he was as ignorant as a kish of brogues.' She looked across at Aunt Bessie and challenged her.

'You said, Bessie, that I'd never abide Cloncon, not after Glen Leven, but you were wrong. I stuck it out, year after year, didn't I, and nobody but Kate and James with me. Now I'm going to give Ann the chance I never gave any of you.'

She was nothing if not a grasshopper. She changed her train of thought in the twinkling of an eye.

'The Dean will make you his special charge, Ann. He says he has found a diamond in a coal mine! "How Green was my Valley", somebody said . . . some famous book. My brain is molasses in January now. I can't remember any more . . .

'In my day a girl was not supposed to be clever. She had to have a good dowry and be able to breed sons and run a house and sew a fine seam and see to the poor of the parish. I was never done with it, and look where it set me, this breeding of sons!'

There was a flash of lightning across her face and maybe we all sat straight in our chairs. James's voice came crystal clear down the long passage from the hall.

'How do ye take salmon from the river outside your bedroom windows. By God! They're like sardines in a tin, when they come up to spawn.'

The Czarina was quite terrifying.

'Dear God!' she said. 'My eldest son, James. James Peppard Hamilton . . . James Peppard Hamilton. I don't know why I gave him the Peppard distaff-side name. If I had it to do again, I'd have christened him Tony Lumpkin . . . Oliver Goldsmith and She Stoops to Conquer . . . and the Inn of the Three Jolly Pigeons. Tony Lumpkin he is and that's what he'll stay . . . cunning but no brains.'

She raised her voice to a shriek. 'I had so many children that I didn't know what to do, but they were all Hamiltons of Glen Leven's . . . never sons that should have been sired on me. When Hamilton killed himself in the hunt, they were all chaff in front of the rising storm. I'd call your Uncle James Hamilton 'Caliban', for that's what he was and still is this day. If I had it to do over again . . .'

I knew she was very angry and was feeling her years . . . 75 now.

'James Caliban Hamilton.'

I imagined Cloncon would have sunk down since the last time we had visited it. Maybe Aunt Katie would have taken to sack cloth aprons and Wellington boots in the house . . . over bare feet. It had been bad enough, when we were small, but I was scared suddenly I stood up.

'I've got to make up my own mind, Grandmother. I will never leave Derrycreevy willingly. We've held it for two years and it can't get worse. I know now that I will never willingly leave Derrycreevy. I'll struggle on here for a while longer. I'll not accept defeat – not yet . . .'

I refused to flinch before the sabre thrust of her eyes . . . so I went on humbly.

'I thank you for your offer of hospitality, Grandmother, but that would be charity and it's kind of you to offer it, but I will never receive charity and that's what it is.'

'You'll have to be told then, Miss,' she said and her voice was a steel trap that meant to hold me and not let me away. 'I didn't want you to be told, but it's all your own fault. How have you reckoned that you and your mother have survived two whole years? I have no patience with you.'

I shook my head dumbly.

'You'd best know it then, hadn't you?'

She let me have it with no mercy, yet I thought she admired me for my last stand of all.

'All the small benefactors of your father's will, they relinquished their claims to his estate. They put their money back in to pay out the debts of Derrycreevy . . . debts, debts, debts. I grant Dinny still wears his watch and Michael his medal, but their small change settled your butcher's bills.

Miss Hamilton's bay mare is still credited to Derrycreevy estate and the trap and the smart turn out. The sailor has never claimed his Admiral Fitzroy's barometer, nor his Captain's decanters . . . not any item of the bequeathed furniture has been claimed. The gels in the kitchen have claimed no penny except for to settle your bills . . . Miss Rohan.'

'You may not know you've been living on charity, child, but you've indulged in doing just that, for two years. You survived so.'

I wanted to put my head down on the table and break into a storm of tears, but instead I drove my nails into the palms of my hands. I smiled at Sarah and Annie and Aunt Bessie and went over to give them all, what they called a bear's hug.

Maw's voice shot a spear through my mind.

'It will all be repaid, Ann, my imperial kitten. I'm your surety for that. Not one of these dear friends will ever know need for the rest of their lives, for what they did for you and my daughter. I'll be your surety, Little Cat. I give you my word and I won't break it.'

I looked at the old lady across the table and her eyes matched mine and there was the same stubborn jut to our chins. There was Peppard blood in me too, but maybe it had not done much good to the Hamiltons of Glen Leven.

'I thank you that you told me what I should have known for myself,' I said, and went to curtsey to her and kiss her hand. 'Thank you for your offer of hospitality too. I hope to come back here in two years and repay my debts for myself. Oh, Grandmother, you must well know the loneliness of "Goodbye". Thank you for understanding so kindly the mess I made of it all. I was supposed to be the ladybird that crept under the warming pan, and I did not recognise it for charity all the time and humanity and great care and kindness.'

Constance Hamilton went off soon after in the clapped-out car with the strapped bonnet. The white woolly dog was left out to exercise himself in the run to the gates. He barked all the way down the avenue and saw to watering the oak trees. Outside the gates, Uncle James halted and waited till the dog thumbed a lift and made Grandmother's silk square a little more grubby. I found I could still smile.

I had worried vaguely about the dog biting Michael or Dinny, but Desmond said they were well able to take care of themselves.

'Tomorrow, I'll meet you at the gate of Cloncon in the evening,' Grandmother said. 'It's a long way over. See that the mare has a cool drink of water and bring bran and oats for her.'

We drove off for the last time, early the next morning, and "Goodbye" was the saddest word I ever knew. Between the outside gates we passed through the golden name plates on the black wood. We trotted off up the hill and out of sight . . . and it was a fine morning . . . Derrycreevy House. Even the plates winked goodbye to us . . . and there was only the hill up the workhouse . . . and the decline by the old gibbet of Gallows Hill.

CHAPTER THREE

'The Meadow of the Hounds'

'Goodbye, goodbye, goodbye.'

Aunt Bessie and I were driving the governess cart to Cloncon with the baggage piled up front. It was a day's journey, but the mare was well up to it. Uncle James had grinned at Michael and Dinny as he drove off yesterday, and had offered some advice on ferrets.

'Don't stuff the animal with food and don't have any fear of him. Gentle as a dove and no harm to him! He'll catch a fine dinner for you and don't be bold in taking the kill off him. Let him see who's master, right from the start. Begin as you mean to go on. Tiger's his name . . . I told you. He answers to it.'

There was a deal of humour floating about, but that morning our morale was rock bottom. The last thing I saw was the brightness of Rohan's brass plates . . . the brightness of the name on the avenue gates . . . and then my tears blurred the grey hill. Their voices sounded still on my ears.

'Goodbye, Miss Baby. Take care how you go. Goodbye, Miss Hamilton and God bless you! We'll mind the house and feed the wild birds. We'll keep the place safe till you come home again, speed the day!'

The mare's hooves sounded a background to our conversation and I was back listening to more of the history of Maw, but maybe I shut my ears to it, for I thought I knew it already.

'Maw married Hamilton because she thought he was like

Young Lockinvar. Her father turned her out, told her to take her things and go, Hamilton wasn't a match for her. There was an earl picked for her, an older man. Then Hamilton snatched her from under his nose, right at the church door and eloped with her. Indeed it was like enough to Lochinvar, but there was no sense in it. They were both too young and they spent money like water. Strawberry Hill didn't want to know.

'I suppose I know as much as anybody of what went on,' said Aunt Bessie.

Then we trotted the miles in silence for a bit till she started again.

'I was the first child and I remembered the lavish way we lived. Glen Leven always seemed to me to be like Vanity Fair. I used to creep out on the landing and look down on the Hunt Balls and the gentlemen in their pink coats and the ladies like a rainbow of colours, but there were too many children. Maw was always expecting another and she would be mad with him, for there was nothing she liked better than riding to hounds . . . and she would want a turn-out of as many of us as could ride out with her . . . and back to Glen Leven then for the drinking . . . and the money running away.'

She remembered it with sadness now . . . the way the nurseries were populated with nursemaids and governesses and Maw most likely sitting in the drawing room at her petit point and very bored, saying her children might well have been steps of stairs – and she could not ride to hounds today.

I knew it had gone on a long time and no healing the breach between Strawberry Hill and Glen Leven. Then all at once it came to an end, with Angus Hamilton thrown on the hunting field . . . carried home dead to the big house.

I wished that Aunt Bessie would talk about something happier, but if I had talked, it would bave been all about the days when we were such a happy family in Derrycreevy, when Rohan had lived an exciting life and carried us on in the tradition of caring. We were so much part of Ballyboy, so much the doctor's children, that people on the street would tell us their troubles and pains and sorrows, expect advice from children, because they had Rohan's blood in their veins.

It was all done now, but I was Derrycreevy and I knew it. If I went, Derrycreevy would go and it must not go. It had lived so many years with a proud tradition.

I snapped myself out of my innermost thoughts and listened to Aunt Bessie.

'James was always a buccaneer, Ann. The lawmen had told us that the till was empty, but the house had a treasure of antique stuff. We had six tenant farms and not half of them paying the rent. We had to get out of Glen Leven, but we owned Cloncon, for it had been the hunt kennels. We might move over to the Whipper-in's cottage, but it was a peasant's dwelling. We might make a go of it . . .

'Oh Ann! I'll never forget it, if I live to be a hundred. I remember thinking that we were like smugglers — James and Kate and I. We got carts . . . six . . . and a hay wain and men we could trust. We ran a deal of the furniture across rutted side roads to Cloncon. We remembered the big barn there. We packed the furniture in one end of it and sheets and household stuff, blankets, china. We piled straw over it all, hid it well. It lies there to this very day. Stuart helped us and Albert too. We got back to Glen Leven at dawn and we moved what was left of the furniture round a bit. There was no man or maid ever told on us and the tax man never knew, but Maw was furious about what we'd done. It could lie in Cloncon as it was, she said. It was Hamilton's not hers. She never wanted to see it again. We had not realised what it would do to her heart to see his chair again and the carpets he had trodden. She was outside herself with anger.'

Aunt Bessie told me never to mention the big barn and its contents, after I came to Cloncon. It was all still there and they could have used it, but Maw would never even talk about it, never even have the lock unturned.

'I wish I had not had to tell you Ann, but you've got to know about it. It's years ago now and I dare say it's all ruined. We'll get by without it, as they've always done in Cloncon. It's a sorry place now, as you'll see and she misses the baying of the hounds across the fields.'

I remembered the laughter that slammed the gates of hell.

'Plenty baying from the woolly dog,' I said. 'I'll have to take him walking and borrow a ferret from Uncle James.'

Goodbye Derrycreevy and Ballyboy and Fergus, goodbye Fergus. I thought of what Rohan always said and how true it was. 'Be sorry for the ones that are left behind. Don't pity the ones that are gone to God's rest.'

'You won't like Cloncon, Ann,' said Aunt Bessie. 'Try to understand it, but you never will.'

As the day went on, the governess car ate up the miles. Once we stopped at a cottage for a cup of tea and some home-made bread. The mare drank from a sparkling brook and I fed her carrots from my hand and let her eat some grass from the long meadow. The evening was coming down as we neared Cloncon and turned off sharply into the rutty muddy lane. The brambles reached for the sides of the governess car as they always did and after a while, round a corner from fifty yards, we saw Grandmother waiting for us, at the gate. The gate was the same old hurdle we knew, fastened with chain on a staple and with hinges of rope. The cattle had made a slough of grey mud that looked as if it might engulf us, in the first gateway.

I had dressed for the journey in jodhpurs and a wind cheater. I had my wellingtons up front and I slipped them on, threw the reins to Aunt Bessie and got out to open back the hurdle. The setting sun was striking gold out of Gran's white head and her eyes were as green as two emeralds. There was no changing anything.

'Goodbye, Derrycreevy. I'll soon be back . . .'

I lifted the hurdle on its rope hinge and swung it back, put my arms about the old lady and kissed the perfection of her papery cheek. Oh God, I thought. Here was Cloncon, where the hounds had chimed music, like bells that rang across the fields.

I was glad of the wellingtons, as I sloshed through the deep grey cattle-tramped mud. My grandmother was wearing wellingtons too and her tweed skirt held up with grace of a lady in a ball gown. She watched me shoo the cattle away and saw Aunt Bessie drive through the gateway. When we were clear of the mud, she released Leo, the woolly dog, and he soon was muddy to his plimsoll line. I picked him up and made much of him and thought what a fall Maw had had from the grandeur of Glen Leven and its chandeliers . . . finally her husband dead and her heart broken. Surely Maw was not to blame.

She was calling to Aunt Bessie to make the mare pick her feet up. I walked off along the rough field at her side and Leo gambolled about me. Then there was another muddy gap and another field and then a post and rail entry to the front garden that was a battlefield of hens. Before I lifted the rails of the front entrance, and saw the concentration camp of fowls, that lived in the garden, I knew that Cloncon was worse than I had remembered it as a child, years ago. I was right, I had slip-slopped through the morass in wellies in the childhood days, but I could exult in mud no more. Here was the no-man's-land . . . hens, geese, and ducks . . . and the duck pond . . . the apple tree that Aunt Kate had grown from a pip. I knew the secret of the big barn now. Here were the trees, where the hens roosted, the hawthorns, the chestnut and the walnut, grown beyond belief. There was a great mass of nettles, that could have been killed by a tin of weed-killer. Here was the pump for water and there was the house at last . . . that a child might have drawn in crayon – three windows across the top – downstairs the front door and two windows. Just any child's drawing. A tiled high tilted slate roof on top. Aunt Kate was waiting on the front steps,

wellingtons on bare feet and a sacking apron and her greying
hair wisping about her face. Her arms were out to me and I
ran to her, felt the cushioning of her bosom, maybe hungry
for the children she would never know. Yet traitor-like, I
recognised the milky smell of the shippon about her. She had
an apron with windfalls in it and a grey donkey at her heels.

'Here's your old friend, Ann, come to see if you remember
that she likes apples.'

Fanny's velvet mouth nuzzled my hand for apples and I
wanted to weep. Aunt Bessie had gone off to stable the mare
at the back and Uncle James came out of a shed at the side
with a forkful of hay over his shoulder and a zinc bucket of
water in his hand.

'A hundred thousand welcomes, Ann,' he cried. 'You're a
sight for sore eyes – with the youth and the loveliness,
shining out of you –'

'Don't you trust him,' the old lady shrieked at him like a
parrot. 'He's always up to tricks, even with his own sisters
when they were half grown . . . fill the bath with cold water
and then deposit the gels in it. I never dare guess what
damage he did to their courses . . .'

She lost me there.

'James Caliban' she cackled at him. 'Is it for our tea we're
to have the forkful of hay, or are you fetching it for the mare?
I see she's to have fresh water at any rate.'

He only laughed at her and said that girls had more shocks
on their wedding night, that might upset their courses right
enough, but Aunt Kate caught my elbow and had drawn me
into the hall and so into the parlour. The old lady went on
grumbling.

'I'll never understand how James is my son, but I saw him
born myself, so I supposed it must be so. He was all
Hamilton and never Peppard . . . Hamilton like a Lepanzer
stallion.'

So I was not going to be kitchen company, I thought, as
the dairy smell followed us with Aunt Kate into the parlour.

She had kicked off her wellingtons and picked a pair of slippers from a pile in the hall.

Here was the parlour then. I remembered it just a little shabbier from the old days. I had never seen Glen Leven and its crystal chandeliers. Was it Aunt Bessie that had told me of the chandeliers at the Hunt Balls in Glen Leven?

The parlour was twelve feet square and the cottage piano with its yellow keys had known better days. I moved from one dumb note to another and another. The tinny notes that did play reminded me in an unholy way of "Boys and Girls come out to play" and the music box and the minuet, so that I shivered.

The old lady nodded her head at an ostrich egg, that stood on the bamboo table, which held the family Bible.

'Stuart and Albert emigrated to Australia,' she told me. 'Albert sent me that ostrich egg after a year or two. I put a great store on it, so be careful when you dust it.'

Her mind seemed miles away.

'It's all I've got left of three of my sons, for John went with them and died almost at once. Then they all took their own way. I get a few cards sometimes and more recently, the next generation call once in a while to have a look at us – don't like what they see and soon go away again.'

Uncle James came in with a great jovial laugh and winked at me.

'Did you ever hear tell of young chicks that come looking for athe pickin's?' he asked me. 'Our young ones come looking to see what remains of the crystal chandeliers of Glen Leven House, time or two. We see them once and never again. This is Cold Comfort Farm, Ann. You'll have seen it for yourself. Up to now, they've slung their hooks at the look of our prosperity and legged it back home as quick as they could. Don't blame 'em.'

Aunt Kate linked her arm in mine, for her mother was taking no notice of her.

'Maw doesn't care any more,' she said. 'I'll never forget if

I were to live to be a hundred. Never forget it . . . I was out that day and Paw was keeping me close by, for I wasn't all that good yet and he knew I was frightened. It was all done so quickly that it wasn't true. I'll hate the smell of the gorse for ever. There was this great double bank came up out of nowhere, on the side of the railway line. It was a big as a house and a narrow jump down sideways into a mean little road. He was minding me to safety and he took no care for himself. Then I saw him lying in the road and his head all to the side. I jumped down off my horse and caught his bridle, before it dragged him, for his foot was still in the iron, Little Ann! It seems strange that you saw your father die too.'

Poor Aunt Kate was caught in sorrow.

'It was the same sort of way to end a life too,' she said.

I was looking up at the oil painting over the mantlepiece . . . the young Bride of Glen Leven . . . a girl on a fine horse, high white stock on her neck, tilted silk top hat veiled. The painter had caught the delicacy of the veil in his painting, and maybe the love Miss Peppard bore for Hamilton. She had been the most beautiful lady and now she was an old woman. I got the crawling of horror in my stomach. I looked straight into the eyes in the portrait and I saw myself in her shade. My chin tilted at her. I outstared two green eyes. I shot out some strange reflected defiance . . . at my own self.

I was shaken. I could not deny it. It was as if I had come face to face with . . . me, a long time after I had been dead. She was beautiful. There was no doubt of that. Even now, the beauty haunted the shadows of her face.

'You're very like her, Ann,' said Aunt Kate in a low voice. 'Out there in the barn, but you know what's there. In here, we live as best we can, peasant style now. James and Maw and me. It's happened to you now . . . the decline and fall of a fine empire.'

After a while, we straggled out to the kitchen, which was on the other side of the hall. It was open plan, just one large room, with a wide fire, lit by turf and logs. There was a range beside the fire and an oil-burning oven stove off away in one corner. Under the window was a big wooden table, where the milk set for the cream to rise. Straight through the centre of the room ran a refectory-type table and wooded chairs. The table was bare of linen and the knives and forks had old fashioned horn handles, the forks double pronged. The crockery was in no way matched. The table might have done very well for 'the rude soldiery', I thought.

There was a flight of stairs that led along the far wall and ended on the first landing. The top storey rooms ran off this landing and the banisters were draped with old rugs and blankets against the draughts of winter, which might soon be felt. It gave the whole place the appearance of a second-hand clothes shop. It was seedy-looking. The floor was dirty and had the look of being a passage to miry wellington boots. It was a depressing place. There was a good supply of house slippers and shoes knocking about and dirty wellingtons, that awaited at each outside door.

Nobody ever came here any more, I thought. They came, but they went away again. I liked the look of the rich cream on the vats, but maybe it was the only richness on the farm.

I whispered to Aunt Bessie that we must change all the standards of Cloncon. She smiled at me sadly.

'Do you think that we didn't try years ago?' she asked. 'Have you forgotten that we turned pirate and we got our lovely stuff from Glen Leven. It's all there still in the big barn, covered with straw against ever being found. Didn't you understand, honey? Maw was crazed with grief. We were not going to let Glen Leven loose in Cloncon. We've never spoken any more about it. That barn has never seen light from that day to this.'

I decided I must get a look inside that barn. Uncle James would help me, but we must pick our time, perhaps get Maw off for a drive into the town with Aunt Kate to do some shopping. It was a matter of strategy.

'Why is the table not properly set?' the old lady demanded

and Aunt Kate murmured that the cloth must be in the wash. It was quite clear that there was no such thing as a cloth in use. I wondered if my grandmother was a little mad. She was certainly eccentric.

'Besides, Ann has not seen the upstairs floor yet, nor had time for a wash,' said poor Aunt Kate.

'She'd do better to have a turn at the pump in the yard,' laughed Uncle James. 'She can get some water up to the tank while she's at it. Our water system ain't all that modern, but you'll learn the knack of it soon enough.'

This was one of his own jokes and he had a habit of joviality about the hard things of life. He left rakes in your path and hoped that they would fly up when stepped on and were aimed to strike between the eyes.

Aunt Bessie was showing me the top landing, her face grim. There were two big bedrooms, one at each end of the landing, Grandmother's and Uncle James's. Two smaller rooms lay between these, Aunt Kate's and then next to it Aunt Bessie's which I was to share with her. There were old feather beds everywhere and white counterpanes, a water jug and a ewer, a marble topped wash-hand stand, the usual things, but very out of date now.

It was all far worse than I had expected, but I had not seen the bath-room. This was a big room with a bath in it and a flush lavatory. The trouble was that it rarely worked. The water had to be pumped up from the pump yard and the flush was full of temperament – bad temperament. Uncle James took a baleful look at the cistern as he went past the door, on his way to his bedroom.

'The damned thing has the evil eye. It goes back on you a time or two . . . no I tell a lie. It goes back on you mostly. It's got to know who's master. Give it a good chuck. If the chain breaks, there's plenty of string about – some wire hidden away too. The water runs rusty an odd time and it's cold, but it all works mostly. If not, there's an earth closet out back if you prefer less muscle work.'

Aunt Bessie and I were alone in our bedroom by this and I wanted to grab her hand and say I must go home, but that was a luxury out of my range by now. I managed a creditable laugh, as I told myself and I told Aunt Bessie too that she and I would bring a change here. 'We loved Rohan and we loved them all, Aunt Bessie. We didn't let Derrycreevy House itself suffer, or I don't think we did. You know that your Maw put her sufferings on an altar and she sacrificed all her children. She let you faithful ones suffer and maybe she didn't even say thanks to you. They went away and didn't want to come back.'

I went on after awhile.

'You and I *must* do something about Cloncon. We must see what's in that barn. Uncle James would help us.'

I jogged at her elbow, but she shook her head.

'James would say "Softlee, softlee, catchee Monkey, Honey". Let's have patience and take this as it comes. I know the flame of your crusades, Little Cat. I'm on your side. Never forget it, but rest tranquil for now.'

They were waiting for us at the table and the old lady very much the empress in the carver chair and the dog on her lap, waiting for his share of bits from her plate.

'Welcome home, Bessie welcome home, Ann Cathcrine. Isn't it high time you came over here to help us?'

I looked down the board at the assortment of china, and the bone-handled cutlery, at the antique Irish silver potato rings – and the potatoes baked in their jackets – the fresh boiled fowl, the rich streaky bacon, the white drumhead cabbage. Gran was carving the fowl, having banished Leo to the floor. James sliced the bacon to the warmed plates, as they were passed. There was a generous slab of bacon and the white cabbage and some very rich sauce. Grandmother was getting rather tangled in her formal welcome to us. Uncle James winked at me, as I tried to reply to the welcome and made no hand of it. For some reason he insisted on calling Leo "Shamus", and I thought it was to ruffle Maw.

'Your mother's daughter is indeed welcome,' he said, as my words dried up on me and again that sideways twinkle.

'What's yours is mine and what's mine's my own, as the Tom Cat said to the Veterinary.'

The old lady shot a malevolent look at him from the head of the table, that should have shrivelled him, except that his laughter was echoing somewhere up among the rafters.

'It may have escaped your attention, James, that you have a young lady guest present.'

He put back his head and there was a joy that filled that house and would not be shut out.

'And how would you think that I might not notice our young lady guest?' he shot off at her. 'Had I not only to go to the drawing-room and look at the portrait of yourself, Madam? You're in there, but she's in there too. Deny to me that Ann Rohan stands there tonight and is back again and I have a great joy about me. God help us all for what life did to every one of us. We're just here in Cloncon, trying to make the best we can of a bad job. Tonight, when I looked at the portrait beyond and then turned my head to see the Little Cat, it was like as if the girl stepped out of the likeness of the most beautiful of ladies. I knew that good luck can come to old houses again. It's my guess that that our bad luck's run out and our good luck running in . . . perhaps not in one great triumph of winning the sweepstake, but multum in parvo – maybe we'll hasten slowly . . . Anyway, however it is, you're welcome, Ann Catherine.'

'Is she like me? Is she? My own dog seems to think so too. I never saw the varmint to take to a person as he's taken to her. You're a nice-mannered girl. I'll say that for you child, but now set yourself down to a good dinner. The fowl was killed three days ago and it's cooked to a turn.'

Suddenly she turned her anger on Kate, her good humour gone as quickly as it had come.

'For pity's sake, why are the lamps not lit?'

Aunt Kate got to her feet wearily and placed two oil lamps

on the table, globe and glass funnel and they were in fashion again. There were two plainer oil lamps for each end of the mantel piece, but all the lamps burned oil. Cloncon did not recognise the Electricity Supply Board yet. It was a very isolated part of the country. The walk of the big electric pylons had stopped short. Here we had oil and candles and turf and logs and coal. When we turned taps for water, that water had been pumped laboriously to a higher level. Even the flush mechanism of the lavatory was possessed of an evil spirit, so that it might "go back on a person". I smiled a little secretly and thought this state of affairs made for peace, like Innisfree and "I will arise and go now". How wrong I was! I knew too soon. I looked at the range and the old oil stove and the piles of turf and logs and coal, and wondered. I had to admire the big open fire with the three legged-pot and the iron double plates, that, put into the open fire, turned out the most wonderful soda bread. I had seen that each bedroom had a candlestick with a fresh candle. There was no doubt in my mind at the moment, that Aunt Kate lived like a wife in a movie about "the women who won the west". Her hands were grey shrimps and she had a beaten look about her. Grandmother's hands were not acquainted with work. They were still the hands of a pampered lady, but they were grubby. There was no denying it. She was addicted to costume jewellery, as if she wanted to fly some defiance flag. Paste diamonds called your eye to look at the beauty of her hands. They were perfection, these hands, but they did no work. There was a green brooch at her neck that maybe was a good luck sign. I never saw her without it. I imagine she pretended it was an emerald. It might have belonged to the wife of the Shah of Persia, but I knew Harrod's crackers when I saw them. It was a good paste jewel. I'll say that. It would have become the best emerald in all the world, if the Shah's wife had worn it. I knew that here was a Shah's wife fallen on the most evil of times and trying to keep her chin jutted. Gems just were not that big and I knew that Gran's

diamonds were paste and her emerald was glass. I felt
terribly sorry for her. She was a kind woman. She had
opened the door to me when the hounds would have eaten
me up. She had given me a strange kind of sanctuary. I was
to have two years of grace to find my feet again. I had been a
spoilt child maybe. I had certainly known a loving home and
I felt so lonely for it that I was maybe destroyed to the depths
of my soul. Just now, I dare not think of the children that
were gone. They were never far away and I thought of them
every odd second and prayed they were in happiness, but
they invested Derrycreevy with themselves. We recalled
them at every moment of a day. If I could just pick up Baby
Alice in my arms, just one more time and see her black eyes,
that had been so full of brightness. If I could just once try a
finger against the sharpness of those new front teeth. One
should be able to control one's thoughts. After all, they were
the product of one's own mind.

Then dinner was over and we were in the parlour at
Cloncon again. Aunt Bessie and I had helped with the
clearing up and the putting away.

'The girl's an example to you, Kate. She doesn't stack up
and leave till after breakfast. You've no right to accept their
help and lounge in the easy chair all the evening. You won't
ever let me help. It seems I'm to be deposed of being the
Mistress of Cloncon.'

In the parlour, she took another keen look at her portrait
and perked up a bit. The portrait was lit by two candles in
Sheffield plate candlesticks, that were worth something in
antiquity.

Grandmother took a sly look at me, when I came in later.
She fingered the notes of the piano and remarked that it was
past time "the pianoforte" was tuned. The sound of the notes
shivered my spine. At any moment, I might hear the music
box out in the moonlit garden and what was it but a wrecked
ghost of itself, this pianoforte?

'There are several notes missing,' Grandmother said

crossly. 'See to it, Kate, when the man comes round again. I dare say the instrument has woodworm in it too, and it's been neglected. Nobody cares any more.'

She closed the lid gently and wrote DUST ME on it with an arrogant finger. Aunt Kate was apologetic.

'It's been dry weather, Maw.'

'And when does a pianoforte object to dry weather, gel?'

There was the ghost of rebellion in Aunt Kate's face.

'I had to pump all the water up to the tank. It didn't rain for months and I had nobody to help with it. You know we can't let the cistern run dry.'

Uncle James changed the subject on purpose in the way I recognised. He addressed Aunt Bessie and myself with full instructions on how to flush the lavatory pan.

'Just grab the chain, when you're done. Give it two or three good chucks, but mind the chain doesn't come off in your hand. Was I not telling you? I have a coil of wire in behind the throne. If it breaks, you can fix it again as good as new. Don't go hard on the whole apparatus or you might have the cistern down on your head. There's a knack in it. The trouble is to get the tank on the roof topped up.'

He sat down on the piano stool and turned himself round on it, announced to the room at large that Mr. James Peppard Hamilton would now have the honour of rendering to the company the tune, that was all in the vogue at the moment . . . "There was I, waiting at the church . . . she left me in the lurch, waiting at the church . . ." 'Sometimes Shamus accompanies me, but he hasn't words yet.'

There was a razor battle between Uncle James and Gran. It was something I could not begin to understand, that night, though maybe I did months later.

We were all laughing.

Then Uncle James, that white knight, had ridden again to the rescue, for maybe he tilted at Gran, but he spoke to me.

'I did tell you that there's an alternative to the high-born cistern. There's an earth closet at the side of the big barn and a pile of logs beside it. If you're afraid to pull the communication cord, take to the earth like a fox. It has an added advantage. It's honour bound to carry one or two logs into the kitchen with you or one or two sods of turf. It's an economic system. It works . . . fuel for the kitchen fires.'

His eyes tried to destroy my misery and maybe his sister Bessie's too.

'It's why the earth closet is called a convenience. It delivers logs or turf on a regular basis. Sometimes, I wonder why the kitchen never suffers from a surfeit of fuel. There's no scarcity. I don't recommend the earth closet myself. My "heads" is between here and the Slieve Bloom mountains. Do I not have the freedom of the whole earth, like the King of Ireland?'

Later, I looked at the painting over the mantelpiece and it caught me up into itself. I tried to ignore the tirade the Czarina of all the Russias was releasing on Uncle James.

There was a look in the portrait that mirrored myself in candlelight.

The Czarina swept out of the parlour to the kitchen with a swish of the long skirt.

'So you've come to be kitchen company, you and Bessie,' she said angrily. 'No more talk about Glen Leven. If we don't talk about it, it will go away.' Her brooch caught the soft light of the lamp, and somehow we had all gathered round the big open fire in the kitchen. Outside an owl hooted and its mate replied from a tree beside it in the garden.

'Don't think of it, Maw. It goes away, as you say,' Aunt Bessie echoed.

The oil lamps on the mantelpiece caught the gleam of the green brooch.

'At least the kitchen is warm and has light. What use is it to hark back?' Gran said.

We had settled down in the shabby armchairs that surrounded the open fire and outside the wind was rising. The woolly dog kept turning round and round in his

blanketed basket and Uncle James said it was a thing he did
when he was looking for snakes in his bed. 'If we don't have
the tea soon, the mice will be trotting across it,' he went on
and quite suddenly I got a great admiration for Uncle James,
for the way he drew his mother's fire, not least in the way he
called the dog "Shamus" which was not his name. Here was
the heir to Glen Leven and no self pity about him. Here
indeed was the man, whom I would require to back me in the
raiding of the big barn. Here was the man, who would enable
me to examine the Glen Leven treasure, if there were such a
thing. At that moment, I made up my mind.

Gran seemed never to take her eyes off me. She apologised
over and over for Uncle James and addressed him as Tony
Lumpkin and Caliban.

Once he looked at her shrewdly and put a hand over hers.

'The best laid schemes of mice and men gang aft agley,' he
said 'and come to naught. At least we can help Ann. Come to
think of it, Ann's had a crash of fine plans. Let's not hark
back to what might have been for all of us. Let's just hope for
a good day tomorrow and that the sun will shine. Let's stick
together. Now it's time we were abed, for we're early to rise.'

I said goodnight to Gran and kissed her papery cheek.
Then I put my arms round Aunt Bessie and Aunt Kate and
at last I kissed Uncle James and thanked him for the good
dinner.

'Why, God bless you, child! You're more than welcome.
You've brought the old house to life.'

I thought that I should run upstairs and light the candles
in the bedrooms, so I went off up the stairs with the woolly
dog at my heels.

'Faugh!' I heard from the Czarina. 'She's emotionally
upset. But who can blame her? Do you really think that your
farmyard manners tonight, James, will make her more at
home?'

Upstairs I burrowed into Aunt Bessie's side in the
feathered bed, as she snuffed out the candle.

'Maybe you forget what it was like here, when you were a little child,' she said. 'Just that complete silence, but for the hoot of an owl or the bark of a fox, and the glory of the cocks as they tell the morning, and no trouble in your mind, for all Derrycreevy stood behind you and as much love as ever a child had.'

I did not answer her, for I could not.

'Two years we have, Honey.'

'Between us, we'll get it better,' I promised her. 'We have each other and we'll be able to throw weight into what Uncle James does and poor Aunt Kate. We have the mare and the governess cart for transport. We'll work at Cloncon all the hours there are.'

Aunt Bessie told me that the Dean had been over and left us work . . . studying work. I had exams to pass to get me further education. There had been an out-building called the "Kennel Offices" on Cloncon, for the old Glen Leven hunt. We must give the place a spring clean right away. The Dean had left a load of books and papers and everything we might need for schooling. First of all, Aunt Bessie said we must get the whole little building spotless. I had not seen it yet, but it was like a University set of rooms. She had had such accommodation once that she would miss it all her life.

'I had to come home. There was no chance of my staying on there or ever going back there again. Maybe I'll recapture it with you.'

Aunt Bessie held me in her arms and whispered in my ear.

'Don't ever look back, Ann. I wasted a deal of time looking back. Now we'll look front. You've been blessed with such an opportunity the ways and means, all to your hands. Say two years of the hardest study and expert guidance from His Reverence. You could take the world by storm . . . the world of higher education. Don't hanker for what's lost. It will get better and better. I'm convinced of it. We must never be selfish, Ann. We must work here as we've never worked and not only at our studies. We'll have to muck in with the pumping of the water up to the roof. We'll have to help milk the cows and collect the eggs and clean the stables. I dare say we'll have to work twenty-five hours in each day, but we'll do it. Both of us have been taken in and no talk of payment, so we will try to pay them a hundredfold.'

The night was silent against the star-lit sky.

'We'll pay them a hundredfold,' I said. 'As God is my Judge.'

I wondered that night, if the recording angel was fast asleep with his beard tucked under the sheet and maybe he never heard me, but I think he did, and maybe he was impatient that people could not see after their business matter in the day, when a man might be awake.

Perhaps I had a pretend conversation with him, while he looked at me severely through steel-rimmed spectacles, half way down his nose.

'Your Highness,' I said to him mentally, for Aunt Bessie was asleep. 'This is another disaster area. You can't deny it. I see it as my duty to help Cloncon to the best of my ability. After all, they're helping me. I know I've come here to try to get higher education, but they're in need, and they're all maybe gone beyond the saving of anything. But there's nothing so bad as that, and Aunt Bessie and I will work hard to get things set right. I'm going to try harder than ever I tried before at anything – to get this house proud again . . . don't know how, but we'll do it. Mark it down in the records against my name. I'll call it "the great endeavour" ' . . . and with that I was asleep.

CHAPTER FOUR

The start of the endeavour

The sun shone the next day and the bees were busy in the garden, that I knew was a no-man's-land for ducks and hens and geese. It would be a quagmire in the winter. I shuddered at the thought of it. It only wanted the banishing of the stock to the back field and a great deal of henwire. Aunt Bessie and I were keen gardeners, but then, in the background at Derrycreevy, had always been Dinny and Michael.

We went downstairs early and found Aunt Kate dealing with a running buffet of breakfasts. You can call it nothing else. It started at half past five when Uncle James went out to do the milking, pulling on his wellington boots and donning an old coat, that looked as if it could be used by a scarecrow. There was a big brown pot of tea on the stove and the table was set with the horn handled knives and forks. There were scrambled eggs steaming in a dish and a tin plate piled with fried streaky bacon and a little basket full of fried bread. The milk would soon be in and then there was work to done. We tried not to be in the way, Aunt Bessie and I. There was cream risen for the churning and the new milk to be put in the vats. There was butter to be fresh churned. Somebody had to collect the eggs and wash them and the speckled hen was laying away, so that meant a search. The water had to be pumped to the roof in case Maw happened to want a bath, or the use of the cistern. Always there was fuel to tote to the kitchen. Aunt Kate was a down-trodden slave. Aunt Bessie and I tried to fill in for her and do her job. At least we persuaded her to sit down and make a good breakfast.

'Never have time for much breakfast here,' she murmured, as I piled her plate with scrambled eggs.

'Leave it to us,' I said and went on a chase of chores and I was not half so efficient as I thought. Uncle James was in for his breakfast now and he was 'a fried egg and bacon man'. I watched him at the table and saw him go through the fried eggs and the fried bread like a circular saw. Aunt Kate had home-made marmalade in the cupboard. I opened back the front of the stove and did toast and piled a stack of it at Uncle James's side with a fresh wedge of butter, and he ate every bit of it, told me I'd make a good wife for a poor starving man, as long as he could bring in the money.

Dear God! There was laughter in the house after a long time.

We even laughed about the hen that laid away. They had found no eggs for a long time now, and here she came stalking into the garden with a brood of chicks behind her.

'I'll set the coop for her,' Aunt Kate said. 'Isn't she the clever one? I'll put her out front under the Solomon's Seal. She'll be able to see us come and go. She likes talking to people.'

We were quite merry, when at last the old lady came down and I think she was surprised at us. She had bathed and dressed in that awful bathroom and the emerald brooch shone from the place where it pinned her cardigan to her dress.

I was back at the range and perhaps she would like a dainty breakfast. I found two fresh brown eggs in the crock and I had boiled them just right. I knew that the toast from the range was super-buttered and piled in small slices and the butter running richly. It was amazing what a sprig of parsley did to it . . . and a late rose from the garden . . . and the fresh butter, just coming in the churn. I did it up in curls and squiggles, and there was a dish of home-made marmalade and I had managed a batch of little Scots scones in the oven.

Maybe the recording angel had heard me, but by mid-morning I was worked to a standstill. This was not a pace I could maintain – but I maintained it.

Aunt Bessie tucked her arm through mine.

'Come and look at your study area, Ann. Imagine you're at Girton College in Cambridge and the whole world of knowledge open to you.'

"The Kennels" was a wonderful place, that had fallen on evil times. The hounds had been housed in the main part of it and this was rich man's territory, the names of some of them still on small brass plates, the relics of 'ould dacency', the barred runs . . . the little unpolished plates, that did not forget.

All were left to silence, Growler and Steadfast and Bellman and True.

The main building was round with a door and two circular windows. There had been no worry about cost in the old days. There was a tall chimney at one end. It had the look of a witches' house . . . circular, twenty feet in diameter, hand made brick the floor of it, just a memory, no more. There was a table and the same wood chairs that they had in the kitchen, shelves, that must have held records, a long time ago. Somebody had been here to prepare for me and I knew the Dean's touch. There were fresh text books piled, fresh reference books and soft-tipped pens, writing paper, a note from my grandmother, stuck up in the paper rack.

'*Dean Matthew Langdon sent his man over a day or two ago and his Reverence says you're to have these things. He came here himself first and looked us over. There was nothing but the best good enough for Ann Catherine. She's to study with Miss Hamilton. It's cosy even in winter, or so I imagine. The chimney draws well and the open grate will keep the life in the place. Pile the wood and the turf against the wall and maybe a lump of coal too, against a hard winter and harder studying. Constance Peppard Hamilton.*'

The open grate was elegant and a chimney stack ran up from it to the roof. It was a wondrous place. I longed to get at it and make it mine and work there without respite. It was a place where one could escape in one's brain.

I stopped myself up short. The Dean had drawn a schedule of studies and the dates of exams, but I could not bury myself here. There was the ship of Cloncon sinking to starboard and it was our duty to see that it did not sink. Added to the Dean's schedule must be scrubbing and polishing, and breakfasts and milking . . . rooms to turn out, beds to be made, stables to be mucked out, the infernal pump to be pumped, so that we could flush the lav . . . if the chain did not break, in which case the chain to be repaired.

'It must be possible,' said Aunt Bessie. 'There are two of us.'

'And there's Aladdin's cave,' I whispered. 'There's all that stuff packed in the barn.'

'You wouldn't dare,' she said, and I laughed at her.

'Me and Uncle James too,' I said. 'You watch us.'

Just for now, I looked at the graceful round windows and the table . . . got the smell of new books and clean fresh paper. The whole room must be cleaned to sparkling bright. In my imagination, I could see it in the snow, maybe two winters away. Somebody had put a swinging oil lamp, hanging from the ceiling and it gave the whole place magic. Grandmother had said it had once hung in the church of Aghancon, where the family graves were. It all seemed to fit in a perfect way.

When we had served our time here, there was Derrycreevy and our plans for it. This was in the nature of an apprenticeship, I thought. Please God I would pass all my exams and aim for the university. I could not see the way clearly, but I was determined to try.

I thanked my grandmother formally.

'I only hope I can repay you for what you have done for me, Madame.'

'Maybe you've already done a great deal for me, Little Cat.'

Maybe we were fools to remember the days when the hounds would meet here and the sheer glory of it. I knew they would have run out across the green grass fields with the chime of bells in their throats, frost in the air and the horses jostling to get on . . . the crack of the master's whip. Hamilton . . . Angus Hamilton . . . Master of Hounds.

'The days are long gone, Ann. You've not lost the heart of youth. Maybe you're a clean frosty wind that sweeps Cloncon just one more time, child.'

She asked me if there was anything I wanted and I told her at once and it maybe pricked all our dreams.

'Hen wire, Grandmother. If it's the last thing I do, I'm going to put those fowls out of the garden . . . and . . . and . . . and . . .'

And again . . .

'I'd be glad if you'd let me take a scissors and clip the woolly dog out. I think that overcoat torments his soul. I think it's cruel to keep him the way he is. A poodle has the brains of ten dogs and they're the most intelligent creatures on God's earth. Let me clip him out and he'll be just like a fleecy lamb. Then maybe he'll go a-hunting . . . and Uncle James shall not call him "Shamus", when his kennel name is Lion of Judah'.

And so it was and it worked well and the days went slowly by and life went on.

First we clipped the Lion of Judah and he was a new man. He became the last of all the hounds of Cloncon and took up ferreting joyfully, haunted me like a shadow and was very happy.

The old lady showed us the six-foot coils of hen wire behind the barn and left us to it. It was called "The Operation of the Moving of the Hen Run" and nothing will allow me to put it on paper. There was a field behind the house and we did the operation, but it was an awful chore. I remember the way I held the poles for Uncle James to drive them in and then the nailing of the netting . . . and last of all the capture of the prisoners. It was a strange thing for me to realise that we had all helped in it, even Maw at last and the newly clipped Lion of Judah. We laughed a lot. It seemed to me that we had laughed the day away and we were all happy. I thought to myself that it was quite impossible that I could be happy. Was I not in trouble and bereavement and never would I be happy again? But I was and the sun as bright as ever it had been. I felt very sad almost immediately and very guilty, but in a few days, Uncle James wanted to build a shed and he was an adept at building sheds with bracken for a roof and some more of these big poles to be held to be driven in. There I was risking my life under the hammer and great praise on me. I was laughing . . . laughing . . . laughing. It seemed that laughter was no longer a strange sound, for Grandmother was to be taken out with the ferret to catch a rabbit for rabbit pie for supper . . . and so it came to be. If I could have caught the scene down in the plantation with Caliban and a ferret in his poacher's pocket . . . with the way Gran was so worried that the Lion of Judah would never surface again. I can see the Czarina of all the Russias, kneeling at a rabbit hole, imploring her lap dog to come back to his mother . . . and the anger she turned on Caliban and myself . . . for teaching the dog "poacher's manners". Then it was all over and my supper in the canvas bag, and Grandmother saying what a brave hunter "her little Leo" was.

'You were right to clip him out, Ann. He's the last of the Cloncon Hounds,' she said. 'God have mercy on us.'

The difficulty was that the work interfered with the studying.

We had scrubbed the "office" when the hard weather came and the fire was lit in the grate. It was a total escape from life. The church lamp, swinging on its burnished brass chains, created a peace, that I had rarely found anywhere. I was never done polishing that old brass lamp. Maybe I treated it as if it possessed a genie in it, that might answer my longings.

'Let me get Cloncon on its feet and then help me with Derrycreevy. Give me the patience to wait, so that the seasons go as quickly as possible, till it all comes right. When the real time has come, help me to put such an effort into Derrycreevy, that we'll bring laughter there too, soon, soon, soon. Derrycreevy was always my first duty, but I've no choice but to let it wait.'

So as it was, Aunt Bessie and I studied late into the night every night and went to bed when we could stay awake no longer. We would come in from the "office" with the frost crackling our feet and grope up the stairs to fall into bed. It would be the wee small hours and at five o'clock it would be time to get up again. Nobody said it was so, but that's what we did . . . and always a dip into the cold water in the bathroom and that was a great awakener, even if the water was still *rust* coloured. Now the weather grew harder and the mornings darker . . . frost in the air, or rain pouring down. I began to appreciate the comfort of a sack apron and maybe another sack cowled over my head. Now I went regularly to help Uncle James with the milking. He was never any different, always cheerful in adversity. I owed him for the hen-run too. Next spring, I would have my garden and soon there would be another spring. There were all kinds of surprises that I found like great gifts from heaven. Christmas roses, and they only wanted a pane of glass to behave as if they had lived in a conservatory all their lives . . . then a year gone and then the small yellow things like buttercups, was it celandines? The winter was on us but the earth was not dead. It was breaking out all over. The bulbs were poking out and then suddenly came the first snowdrops . . . and tears on my cheeks. Slowly they came one after another, all the glories of the violets and the primroses and the cowslips again, but they were later. There had been no such delights the first day I reported to the cowshed for work. It was a filthy day with a north-easter and the rain coming steadily. There was nothing to recommend such a day, except Uncle's ruddy face in the gloom of the lantern and the whiteness of his grin.

'My! Isn't it cold?' I said and the hurricane lamp was trying to persuade me it was making a winter famyard scene, in oils.

'Excuse my cold hands on your bosom,' said Uncle James, from the dusk, 'as the milkman said to the shy heifer.'

He laughed in his usual uncouth fashion and I was glad that his mother was still warm in her bed. I wondered if the Dean would have approved. Yet somehow I knew the rather vulgar humour was at best a lance against despair. I had thought to be very unhappy. I found laughter in the shipon in the small dark hours, with my wellingtons skidding in the muck. It did not seem to matter that I had shrimp hands now, but I was sorry that Aunt Bessie had to have them too, though she took it as the ordinary thing to have. I remembered the time at the college in Dublin, when I was all set to be a lady. It had been a miserable episode in my life. I had to search round now, for laughter things. There was the evening when the Lion of Judah laid a dead rat at Gran's feet, as we all sat before the kitchen fire. There was a shocked silence and then such a burst of laughter.

Maybe we were winning against the stagnation of Cloncon. Maybe we were inching forward. There had been such a lively argument. The rat was two feet in length from nose to tail and there were two courts of opinion. "Shamus", as Uncle James had it, had found him dead, but of course, Maw would not agree. Who dared say that Leo had caught it post mortem? We agreed with the Czarina after a time. It was dangerous not to. It was such an important item of our daily goings and comings and thereafter, we all called him 'Leo, the ratter', but if I wanted to be foolish, I could have given evidence that the rat had rigor mortis and a coat of frost . . .

It was so funny . . . so very funny, in this household of peasants . . . and he was a game little dog, come to think of it, even to think of carrying home a frozen monster . . .

Yet never all through that long winter could we find

courage to ask Gran if we might open the barn. Secretly we might discuss ways and means, but we were so busy that there never seemed time to find. There was no doubt about it that the Czarina was a pillar of stone. We all recognised it. If Angus Hamilton had come riding down the field to the gate, maybe there would have been some means of wakening her. Somehow, I did not believe she was awake nor that she even tried to awaken. She could smile and she could laugh, but she never seemed to live.

As it was, it seemed that always she watched me and I had no idea of the thoughts in her head. I think I reminded her of the days when she was my age now. There was a sadness about her that filled me with compassion for her. If I could have created a miracle, I would gladly have done it and had Angus Hamilton come riding up to the gate, but I've said that before and what purpose is there saying it again? Angus Hamilton was gone for aye, and would never come back, even if the lamp of Aghancon church possessed fifty genii.

We had visitors from time to time. Dinny and Michael and Annie and Sarah came sometimes, the Dean often, Mrs. Cluny once and then not again. I wrote letters to Fergus, but he was on the other side of the world and engrossed in his career. He would not be on leave for a long time, but he was delighted to hear I was so happily settled. He had got heavily involved 'in the third world', whatever that meant. He sometimes wondered if there were such places as Derrycreevy and Gorse Hill House. Had it all been a sweet dream?

I thought of Surg. Lieut. Cluny in tropical kit and all the entertaining, when they docked in port. I had sharp pangs of jealousy, but Fergus did not seem to belong to Cloncon. He maybe had slipped over the edge of my world.

In the second spring, we all started at the garden and found so many things that still were not lost. The paths were sound now and one could walk dry shod and the floors of the kitchen were muddy no more. We were winning at last. It was obvious and we were thankful.

The months slid by and I was studying to exhaustion. I had been for the jump of an examination in the end of the first year, and had cleared it. Back again, I started off again at the beginning of a new syllabus and it seemed that maybe I was half way there, but back in Cloncon again . . . and the cows for the milking and the butter for the churning and the water to be pumped to the roof every day and now sometimes, I rode the bay mare over to the post-office to collect the mail. Cloncon was very isolated. The coal-man was the only tradesman who braved the rutty, thorny-hedged muddy lane. The small sub-post office was three miles away across the fields and there was a shop there. I could fetch the post and the messages there some mornings, but letters were few and far between. In time, the postman would deliver a batch of post, but it was a hard chore for him and I liked the ride, liked the cup of tea they gave me at the shop and the friendly chat of civilisation.

The fetching of the oil was a demon I hated. It was the same sort of task as the pumping of water to the roof tank. We had to have running water and a lavatory pan, so we had to pump up enough water for the supply. I said it made us semi-civilised and it was worth it, but I could feel the earth closet might be a great temptation to use in old age. Maybe one just stopped caring. It could happen. I knew it.

Anyhow, the ride to the post was a bright spot in life. Mostly there was some little thing to fetch and it was a treat for the mare too. She was a splendid bay, with black points and she gleamed like a tea leaf and rubbed her nose against me.

Always I groomed her to perfection and polished her hooves and we kept her clipped out. She was a mount that anybody could be proud of. I imagined myself riding her, Miss Rohan of Derrycreevy House, Ballyboy. Presently, if things had gone right, I might be going the circuit of gymkhanas and putting her at the fences and the double bank, might be winning all before me and parading at the finale, before the judges with the red rosette in my teeth and pat to the mare's neck . . . and the smell of the summer trampled grass.

It was a pipe dream, and often I dreamed it, but it was not for me. It would be a good day if only there was any post. It was a super day if I had a letter from Annie or Sarah. It was none of these things that day, for I'll remember it for ever. It was a letter form Fergus. It was 'the best'.

In politeness, I had to eat my slice of seedy cake and drink the cup of tea and I had to make sufficient conversation, so that the postman's wife was not offended with me. Yes, the roses were all blooming and the red heifer had had a calf . . . bull calf. I had brought the post lady some of the 'beestings of the milk for a custard'. Mr. Hamilton had got his corn out with the stuff the post lady had sent him and was very grateful. The mock orange blossom was filling the whole garden with its scent again this year.

I had a pile of old Dickens books. I'd bring them over to her if she wanted them and I thought she might start off on David Copperfield. It was the best one to start on . . .

'A letter from Fergus. A letter from Fergus. A letter from Fergus . . .'

So Fergus was on his way home perhaps?

There was a sheltered wood half way home with a ruined ancient keep, where I stopped to read my mail. It had a conversation of jackdaws about it and maybe a sheep or two, looking at me out of witches' eyes.

'Dear Ann Catherine . . . I'm on my way home . . .'

It was the second spring and the sparkling of a day. Fergus was coming home, not for weeks yet, but my heart was pounding in my chest. There was a clear pool of water in the keep and I let the mare drink, watched her questing nostrils break the mirror and thought of the Lady of Shalott I had no time for looking in the mirror these days. Before the mare shattered the glass, I thought it quite possible that Fergus

would not recognise me. It had been such a long time. There
had been two winters surely and this should be the last one.
Somewhere along the way, I had lost a winter. I was a
woman now, but when I went to Cloncon, I had been a girl.
The girl of Derrycreevy was quite gone. How had I lost her? I
should have known that the clothes I had got for my fine
Dublin College were all outgrown. They were shrunken and
past the letting out. My wardrobe was utility but adequate
. . . jodhpurs, dungarees, thick-knit socks . . . double-knit
sweater and another for spare, knit by Aunt Bessie in a
roll-top.

My face no longer was youth's face. Even my hair was
different. Ah, yes, the black fringe of it, but the rest of it was
in a pony-tail for utility, held by a bootlace to tidiness. I was
all ankles and elbows and eyes. My breasts were stretching
the last jumper, making it too tight and too short.

I had to admit there was a look of work-house waif about
me. Even with the exercise and the good food, I had a touch
of starvation about me too, a depth of dark sorrow, that
might have come to stay. I missed the boys, who used to
come out to play. Nobody will ever know how much I missed
them, but I was too old for play now.

The mare had finished her drink and had moved on to
fresh grass. My mirror settled again and I made plans. Next
time I went in to town I must buy some new cord jodhpurs,
maybe two pairs. I must unravel the wool of the sweaters and
make two into one, that might be loose on me. I felt so full of
happiness that I thought that maybe the blood was fizzing
like champagne in my heart.

'One fine day he'll come again . . .'

I was Madame Butterfly, if only my voice could raise the
beauty of Puccini. I put the letter carefully in my pocket and
sat off for Cloncon. At least I must ride home in style. I took
the fences one after another, holding the mare's nose to
Cloncon. In my head were galloping all the noble horses,
that had ridden the rides in the days gone by, had taken this

same path all those years ago. The old lady was delighted to see me come home in such good spirits. She gave me a wave of her scarf and the Lion of Judah streamed off to meet me and reprove me for leaving him behind. Uncle James lifted his head from some post he was repairing in the front fence and gave the rebel cry from the war in *Gone with the Wind*. He took the mare from me and said he would walk her up and down, till she cooled off.

'And what news have you had to make you in a sweat too?' he asked me and Gran gave a small lecture about ladies never sweating.

'Ladies glow,' she told Caliban and he grinned at her and asked was that so.

'So Fergus is coming home,' said Aunt Bessie softly . 'He's on his way home at last.'

We all got into a huddle about Fergus's visit, though there was a long time to wait. Aunt Bessie lost no time in washing my hair in rain water and it was the old nursery days come back again. Gran ran her hand through my drying hair and said there was nothing like soft water for a lady's hair, but the boot lace would not do. She had some black watered silk ribbon by her and I must have it.

'You're a woman grown now, Little, Cat. You mustn't dress like the rag-picker's child.'

My wardrobe was replenished. I got the new jodhpurs and we knit up a splendid black sweater, with a loose turtle neck and there was room for all of me in it. I was hardly likely to grow any more, they all agreed. I worked on my hands a bit, or perhaps the whole house worked on my hands. I did not care, or professed that I did not. I was unashamed. If hard work meant that a lady had shrimp hands by necessity, a man worth his salt would understand.

Grandmother advised me to rub lemon into them at night and wear cotton gloves and cold cream.

I grinned at her and said I'd use some of Aunt Kate's cold cream.

'Her hands have lasted out,' I smiled. 'She has the most useful hands I know.'

Grandmother looked ruefully at her own hands on her lap, speckled and freckled with age, the veins blue and prominent. It was one of the days when she had the costume jewellery on and I wondered if she thought she fooled anybody. The green brooch was by far the favourite and it was not even clean. She cackled at me like a demented cockatoo, when I told her I would shine it up in Lux suds and get it really lovely.

'That emerald must be handled with care. It's always gone to Weir's in Grafton Street to be cleaned professionally. One of these days I'll send it off to them. They know what should be done to it, can't have any Tom, Dick, or Harry meddling.'

She snatched it out of my hands and then apologised to me.

'I'm sorry, child. I know you meant to help, but it was a relic of the things I lost. I told you not to touch it.'

God knows I had tried to get her looking smarter. I had sewn on all her cardigan buttons, washed the cardigans and pressed them. I had laundered innumerable silk squares, mostly for "the Lion of Judah".

'That emerald is a talisman to me . . . a good luck piece. There was an old Tinker woman one day in the kitchen and she told me never to leave it off my costume. She said a strange thing . . . said I'd never be short of fine sons and daughters, but I'd be short of luck to the end of my days. She was a rogue like they all are.'

She smiled at me and thanked me for "trying to keep her decent". I had even put lavender bags in her wardrobe, she said, and I had brought back the days to her mind, when her own nurse had made her small self stitch lavender bags.

'I can still smell them in the cedar-wood tall-boy and the sewing was spotted with my blood. I scolded my nurse about it and told her that such a small miss should not bleed to sew seams. Maybe I did not realise that blood must be shed. I was a spoilt miss, Little Cat. I think that Rohan had more sense than Peppard had in the way he brought up his ewe lambs at Strawberry Hill . . . My father promised me that I'd never want for anything, as long as he lived, but he had a change of heart'

She was nothing if not eccentric. I imagined that she was getting worse, but maybe I saw more.

'Men are deceivers ever,' she said now. 'When your Fergus comes home, perhaps he'll have a wife in every port and no memory of the lassie from Derrycreevy, for all that she's a woman grown.'

I was worried about this matter myself. I had changed so much. I had promised to do so much for Derrycreevy, but I had had to lay it all to one side. Even if I did manage to get it restored to the old style, there was this new doctor in Ballyboy. He was quite happy as far as I knew in his new little bungalow on the hill. Why should I pray for God to send me St. Luke? Was it just that I was missing Rohan, for I missed him sorely?

'But if I got Derrycreevy a little bit better,' I prayed, 'and St. Luke took it into his head to listen to me . . . it's no good pretending that I had Fergus in my heart as a doctor for . . . never mind what for . . . Fergus is tied to the Navy. He could not with honour throw it all up and come home to practise in Ballyboy. From every generation comes at least one Cluny son. Oh, God! I can't ask you to change the planets in their sphere. Cancel out the whole prayer. I must not ask what is impossible even to God. I am just the least of things, and almost asleep too, like Father Gilligan asleep upon a chair.'

I counted the days and they were crawling away so slowly that a time or two, I tore off the calendar twice. There were weeks left yet and it was the day to fetch the oil from the town. It was a task we all loathed. It meant taking the black cob in the cart with a cross board to sit on, on a dry sack. The oil drums were monsters. Aunt Kate was dropping with tiredness. Aunt Bessie was spring cleaning the bedrooms and after that there was the flue of the range. Uncle James was loading cattle for the English market at the railway up the line.

Grandmother would oversee everything and that meant that she would hope it was a fine day and she could sit in the garden and watch the honey bees, only it was too late in the year for bees now.

It was not going to be a nice day. There was no sign of blue sky and a north-easter was reminding us of another winter on its way to come. I must go home to Derrycreevy, but just for now it was going to be one of those days, that have nothing to recommend them. There was a small mean rain drizzling down, as I got Tim, the cob, out of the stable and yoked him in the cart. I was dressed in my worst and most outworn clothes. By evening I would be oil-stained and stinking of the wretched stuff. My slacks were too small for me and my sweater had shrunk past the small of my back. I had a tatty yellow oilskin coat and my bare feet were pushed into wellingtons. Either there was a fresh leak in my boots or the rain had topped them up a bit. It did not matter on oil days. The oil was king. It would infiltrate everything. Nothing must be spoilt. That was important, not the half side of pork, nor the sack of maize, not the sugar, not the soap . . . not the "exports" and these were the chocolate that Aunt Kate made for market, the trays of eggs, the fowls plucked and prepared for the table . . . not the home-made butter.

We lived on a small margin and I had learnt it. It mattered very much if any item was spoilt. We laughed at short commons, but there were days when we knew short commons, because some item at the market had not sold. It was a damned serious business and I was honoured to be let to see it.

For the cob, I had put in a nosebag of chaff and maize and oats. There was a bundle of hay keeping dry under the tarpaulin. Tim talked to me with his ears, along the road to the market town and I let him have the benefit of my philosophy.

'It's a terrible day, Tim, but we'll soon be finished and home and I'll give you special warm bran mash tonight . . . and maybe a Mars Bar.'

I went on to tell him all about the electricity.

'We can have it soon, Tim, perhaps not for years, but soon you'll see. The oil is a must, for we *must* have it, but it's the same with the water tank on the roof and the pumping of that cistern. It's tedious, Tim. I know you understand when the stable leaks, but we've fixed that now and it's not as if you aren't a very good horse, for you are . . . don't know what we'd do without you. You may see how close the pylons are coming from the Electricity Board. They're near enough for a miracle soon. Then Tim, what larks! We'll kinda walk on the moon in Cloncon. You'll just turn on a switch and there will be light and all the miracle of electricity . . . vacuum cleaner and maybe automatic washing machine and electric power enough to move the earth.'

The cross roads at Timna Cross was coming up and we were half way to the market town.

'If only we had the Shannon Scheme, there might be a new heaven and a new earth, Tim, but a warm bran mash is a warm bran mash and you'll have one tonight and a dry stable deep in yellow straw . . . and a new salt lick and some mangolds, fresh sliced.'

The black ears talked back and forth to me.

'It may not be so long as you think, Little Cat.'

The rain started in earnest then and I spread the old green waterproof over his broad back.

'You wouldn't believe the difference it makes in living,' I told him and he shook the rain out of his mane at me, so I fed him a few carrots. He went along briskly for the next few miles, till we were at the arch of the market square and I got him through the arch into the inn yard and into a dry stable. He was glad to rest and glad to be out of the rain and carrots were carrots and maize was maize and just a handful of oats was luxury. I got his ears dry and warm and left him to his nose bag.

I had dropped off the oildrums at the shop. They would put them full in the cart later. Then I went the round of all the messages. I was glad when the home produce was safely delivered and then I collected the shopping. My wellingtons were sloshing the water through my bare toes and my hair was soaked and somehow leaking water through my collar and down my neck. I had collected money and I buttoned it carefully inside my coat. It was a good market this week. I thanked God. There had been enough to pay for the half pig and it was safely loaded on the cart, where the oil could not ruin it. Then Uncle James wanted a sack of maize and it was loaded too and well protected against the weather. I almost forgot the new wicks for the lamps, the 4711 for Gran, the chocolate dog drops for "Shamus" as Uncle James would call him. It was the usual oil-day routine and I knew I reeked with oil already and was dishevelled and untidy and the rain running out of me.

It was always the same. The damned drums leaked, but at least they were loaded. I squelched up the small main streets and knew hunger. At the fried fish shop, I bought a delicious bundle of smoking fish and chips wrapped warmly in white paper. I went back to the inn and well I knew that I should not eat such "manna" in the street. The smell of them was so delicious and they were not too hot, just perfect. I ate two chips and then two more and shovelled up a slab of crispy fish.

'I'll meet you outside when you're ready to go home,' Ned, the Boots, had said and he was as good as his word. I gave some chips to the cob, for he had polished off his own food. The Boots was watching me hungrily so I let him have a share too. I knew I should have tipped him, but I had no money, not even enough to bring home presents for Cloncon.

Ned helped me up to the cross bar and gave me a dry sack

to sit on. He thanked me for his share of the fish and chips
and told me to take care how I went.

There was a long red sports car coming much too fast
down the hill for a market day . . . a girl at the wheel with no
care for animals, that crowded the town. She wore a scarlet
scarf that did not cover her golden hair . . . jack wheaten hair
it was. She was beautiful . . . a kind of girl-of-the-year
advertisement for the gleam that fluoride toothpaste might
bring. She went into a sideways tank skid and stopped up
short. Then she looked at me and looked at me again under
the long dark lashes.

The devil was in her eyes and I recalled the sheep in the
keep, the morning I read Fergus's letter. She had witches'
eyes.

'Ann Catherine Rohan! It must be. You were a sprog at
Alex House a few years ago, but you've grown up. Maybe
you've grown down like Alice in Wonderland. Derrycreevy
House it was, in Ballyboy. Alex gave me the sack because my
father was in the red with the fees. We were sisters in
affliction, for you were in the same difficulties. What the hell
happened to you? You look like a tramp and I don't mean a
tramp girl. I mean a common unkempt tramp.'

I sat and looked at her with the paper of fish and chips
warm in my lap . . . could think of nothing to say, wondered
if I should offer her some fish and chips and decided not to. It
might not be the done thing to eat in public, sitting on the
cross board of a common cart.

Then I saw the dark man at her side, blue linen slacks, silk
white cravat, sailcloth jacket navy style. It could not be
Fergus come home too early. God have mercy on one poor
tramp! It was.

He took me in with one keen look from top to toe, every last
bit of misery that was I . . . the loaded cart, the shrunken
clothes, the yellow oilskins, the bootlace that had come loose
from my hair and got mixed up with the fish and chip paper
. . . the tweed cap, pulled well down over my right eye.

'Ann,' he said. 'Ann of Derrycreevy.'

The girl's face was red and she spoke without thought.

'You're the roller-coaster crash girl. You lost all your people. Then Alex had the budget in mind and gave you the shove. I'm sorry for you, duckie, but you're a fool or else you ought to have changed your legal man. You could have taken that fair for a fortune. All you wanted was a sharp silk. No negligence my eye! That Big Dipper was made of three-ply and not serviced properly. If I'd been your mum, I'd have taken it to the High Court. I'd have got millions out of them. I'd have ruined them, but I wouldn't have ended up in a clapped-out cart, trading in the country markets . . . for bread to live on.'

'Shut up, Jill,' Fergus said sharply and got out of the car by dint of jumping over the passenger door.

Still there seemed nothing to say. I held out the fish and chips and he took some of them and then worried in case he had taken too much of my dinner. There was an awful tension, that built up and it built up and up in the small unimportant market street. There was a sheen of prosperity that surrounds an Aston Martin and people were pushing to stare. This then was the end of my dream of Fergus. It was just bad luck that I had not picked a better day . . . not an oil day, but some time when I would have been respectable in the governess cart, with new jodhpurs perhaps and the watered silk black ribbon and my hair as neat as ninepence.

I was not so sure of my dream of Derrycreevy any more. Derrycreevy was sleeping and perhaps it was waiting for ghosts that were gone. At any rate, Fergus had not waited. He had found himself a dolly bird. Mrs. Cluny might have produced Jill for him and maybe she was right. I recognised Jill now and knew her from Castle Wellington in Rocrea. A chap's mother might approve of her. It was a great pity that I had come into the market dressed in my hard-weather clothes, but if I had worn the new things, this day would have taken the newness and made nothing of it. I wanted to hold my face up against the cruelty of life. I wanted to howl against the grey sodden skies.

Fergus was taking the silk cravat off his neck and had made a noose of it round my neck, tightened it, straightened it, tucked it into the neck of the oilskins. He held me as if on a lasso and looked at Jill.

'This is as far as I go, Lady. Thanks for the lift from Ballyboy. Maybe you didn't understand I was looking for Ann . . . didn't expect to find her so soon. I fell in love with her a long time ago. I'm not one to change my mind.'

My brain was like a kitten with a tangled ball of wool. I glanced at Jill and saw that she must have got a nasty message, for her smile was gone and her face was ugly. Fergus had gone to feed some chips to the cob and the cob turned his head round to watch me return to the scene of his vision. Fergus had helped himself to the last of the fish and I thought that his mind might be troubled, for perhaps it was a bit greedy and Jill had been offered nothing and Fergus was taking his time to set the cravat right at my throat again.

'This is as far as I go,' he said carelessly, 'I'll take Ann back to Cloncon now.'

Jill was collecting me in the witches' vision of her eyes.

'Can't understand why you wear that gear. Is it the latest on the ski runs? I don't imagine you got it in Grafton Street. If you've got to fetch that oil all the way to Cloncon, maybe you should send yourself to the drycleaners now and again. Oil stinks.'

'Goodbye, Jill,' Fergus said again. 'It was great of Mother to invite you to meet me, but tell her I've no wish to see you again. I think with luck, I'm spoken for.'

By dint of pulling the cravat, he brought my face down to his. His mouth rested on mine and he took me into his arms. I remember the hardness of his chest against my breast, knew that his heart thudded as fast as mine did. The car was up and away in a great surge of anger but I do not think he noticed it. I knew it had too much speed for the turn at the top. There was an agony shrieking of tyres and the Aston Martin was gone, but still all about us was the business of the market and the cob still looking round at me to see if I was out of my mind. There was a new joy in me. Fergus loves me, I thought, and Fergus was climbing up into the cart by dint of putting a foot on the axle. I shared the sack on the crossbar, but Fergus was careless about it. The people were pretending not to notice, that a strange man had kissed Miss Ann of Cloncon, but they were all wondering what the old lady might think of it.

'Oil is the devil,' said Fergus as if the rain was not pouring out of the skies. 'Anybody that dresses for a garden party when they have to fetch the oil is an awful fool.'

He took the reins out of my hand and took charge of the equipage.

'Anyway the pylons are on their way at last. Did you see the *Irish Times* this morning? It's only a matter of time till they're within reach of Cloncon. Then there'll be a New Jerusalem. It will transform life for farmers like Caliban. Just imagine what electricity could do to the Meadow of the Hounds. It will make all the difference to them and you've been very patient. I think the time is coming when you can be selfish enough to look after Derrycreevy . . . and maybe my poor self . . .'

We came past the fish and chip shop again and he was out of the cart in a moment and had restocked the ship. He had even borrowed a tarpaulin to shelter both of us very comfortably. He had made sure the mare was covered from neck to rump and was happy enough to face the journey home. We shared the provisions between us and we never noticed the rain all the road home to Cloncon, for I had discovered an enchanted place, where time went by like lightning and the sun shone although the rain still poured down.

Maybe it was an echo from the Celtic Carpet.

'Here this! Hear this! Fergus is home.'

'You're Derrycreevy, Ann, always will be. Maybe I've been Gorse Hill, but I'm for you and you're for me, since time began. It was meant to happen the way it did. We'll never understand it, any more than the big trout in the river understands it. Nothing will put you and me asunder. Nothing on God's earth. Just don't forget me. I've got nothing to offer you at this moment of time, but one day I will have. I swear to you. I'll stand face to face with you and all the insoluble problems will have fallen away, like the timbers under a launched liner, as it goes down the slips to breast the seas. I think we'll have a hive for the honeybee in Derrycreevy, you and I. You're Derrycreevy and always will be and I'm Gorse Hill, right to the end of the road. There's nothing to come betwixt us . . . nothing . . . but a river. As I said, we'll never understand it, any more than the big trout in the river understands it, but he has been treated with honour. You must admit that none of us dared to catch him, for he was the king. One day, there will be nothing any more to keep us asunder . . . and we face to face.'

After a while he went on

'Yes, I think we'll have a hive for the honeybee in Derrycreevy and nine bean rows and who will eat so many beans? Think of the bee-loud glades of the oaktrees and know that here we will live happily after. We're two of a kind, Ann. I've always known it. Nothing in God's world can ever destroy us . . . Ann . . . Ann . . . Ann . . . my darling.'

CHAPTER FIVE

The secret of the barn

There had been a time, when I might have been ashamed to introduce Fergus into Cloncon, but not any more. For one thing, we had all worked very hard, especially through the second winter, and now Spring was here. We had a garden instead of a fowl concentration camp and we had changed the house itself in so many small ways. The kitchen was rather a show piece. The range was a thing of old beauty and comfort, burnished with blacking and emery paper. The coal scuttle and the log barrel were old copper, gleaming in competition, one against the other. Fergus was not the sort of man, who would have objected, if we had a new-born lamb in a box near the warmth of the stove, and the bottle with what Uncle James called the lamb's tit wrapped in a warm towel, ready to hand. This was a life that might have never been lived at Aston Martin level . . . and best of all Aunt Bessie had taken the dinner table into her care. We had tablecloths and table mats and matching plates and dishes. It was something she had kept for her bottom drawer and she was old now and past marriage.

'You're welcome,' she said. She had provided a grand canteen of cutlery and matched set of pyrex plates and dishes. 'Why leave them to become useless?'

I was responsible for the scrubbing of the floor and the excluding of muddy boots and the cleaning up of the garden paths.

I was proud for the scrubbing of the floor and the laying of some cheap nylon stuff that lasted for ever. It was in a new synthetic material. It was dark red and hardwearing and it cost very little. I was so proud of the sheep-skin rugs, that I had cured with Uncle's help, in salt in the sun . . . safe dried. They were my pride on the floor of the kitchen. They could be washed and dried as easy as handherchiefs and I was proud of what we had made of the set-up. Yet the portrait was in the sitting room and there was pride there too. The portrait had had some attention with soap and water and it was superb. Uncle James had even put a silver candelabrum under it and it was elegant, and the old piano did the best it could.

So my lamb-skin mats were up-stage and I kept them immaculate. The vats of rising cream were still an attraction, but where was Fergus to sleep?

There was the office of the Cloncon hounds and a fire burning and a divan couch that Aunt Bessie and I sat on, and a warm horse blanket in a silent night. That was Cloncon till the cocks split the night with the dawn and woke him up.

Maybe I jibbed a bit about explaining the secrets of the tank on the roof, but he took it in his stride. He would take his watch on the pumps, he said.

'I'll use the cistern with care, too. Dear Ann! All we want is an electric pump on the well. Given a very little money to spend, this could be a model farm. There's fine grazing here for English beef. This farm could be put on its feet with the right management.'

There were committee meetings under my nose and I never knew it. How could I? Uncle James and Aunt Bessie and Aunt Kate were all avid for discussion with Fergus, but I was cut out. I listened by accident to the daddy discussion of them all, the one between Fergus and Grandmother.

Fergus had sought Grandmother out for a talk, I noticed that everybody had cleared off, yet I did not diagnose the importance of it. Fergus was apologising to the Czarina.

'I'm afraid you'll ask me to leave, when I've said what I've got to say, Madame. You've treated me as an honoured guest and you've made me come happily home.'

Grandmother was putting herself out to please him. Maybe she had just realised all that had happened at Cloncon. Everybody had gone except Aunt Bessie and she was signalling me to get out too. I did not know what was afoot, but Fergus was in the seat by the kitchen fire and Gran was in the old chair in the ingle, her toes to the glowing turf. Maybe Gran had just realised that her kitchen was a show-piece and the cooking superb. Fergus was making up the fire now, for it was a chilly night.

I had to make myself scarce, but where? The top landing was a whispering gallery and my door open. I wanted to run downstairs and tell Fergus to shut up before he destroyed us all, yet he was doing it so gently. Not one of us had dared to do it till now. Yet there was steel in his voice too.

'They have all talked about it,' he said. 'I know the whole story.'

I doubt if he did. There was no need to make Herself sad with the raking of dead ashes. She had lost her whole wealth and her happiness. She had come to live in poverty.

'We came to live like pigs,' Gran scowled at him.

'They would be lucky pigs, that lived as well as you do now,' he laughed at her.

He took his time making up the fire and after a while, and she still scowling at him, he said that there was a balance to such things.

'It's like a ship at sea, Madame. It's tempestuous. It's calm. It's quite clear to me that it has been very rough for a long while, but things are better now. Maybe the battle is nearly over.'

Fergus worked round to what he called "the treasure in the barn", and here her back stiffened.

'I know what's in the barn,' he said. 'I know that treasure was stowed there, safe under the straw, but the roof of the barn is suspect. It's shipping water. I've had a look at it and it smells of dry rot and decay. I can't get Miss Havisham out of my mind – she of *Great Expectations*, and the bride cake and spiders that ran in and out.'

'Ugh!' she said, and I went further on the landing and tried to get the courage to go down the stairs and take her in my arms.

His voice was barely audible.

'You were in deepest sorrow. Perhaps you still are. I can understand how you'd never want to see the riches of Glen Leven any more, not with Himself gone for aye.'

'Can you understand it? Can you indeed? Then you've got an old head on young shoulders.'

'Be kind to me,' he said and his voice was so soft that he could coax the birds off the trees, as she knew for herself.

There was a long silence and then he got on with it and I had my hand on the top of the staircase, ready to go, if I could but get the courage.

'I want you to think of the Little Cat and the changes she has brought here, but have you ever looked at her and seen what these two years here have done to her? She's stood up to more sorrow than ever you've had to do. She's the Ladybird with all her children gone. Her mother and father have gone and her house is teetering on a cliff. She never complains. She works like a slave. She studies into the early morning and she's inching her way up the ladder to certificates of education. She's aimed for the university now and she's lonely for home. She refused to leave Cloncon till it's right for you and that's still ahead. I'd take her out of here tonight, if she'd go with me, but she'll not leave you, till you're happy. She's refused me. I asked her. Now I know that there's maybe a heap of treasure in that barn and I want the key to it. It might release Ann back home to Derrycreevy House.'

There was a pause of perhaps five minutes.

'Madame, there's a hole in the roof of your barn and the weather has likely made a Satis House of its contents. At least let me look. Don't break your heart, if it's only in your memory now. I think you've let it fly away from you and no blame to you, but we'd best know.'

The fire had started to burn up brightly and he put his face in his hands.

'Let me deal with it. I'll give you a true record and maybe there might be that treasure that might let Ann go home earlier. Think of the Ladybird, proud because she's got a watered silk ribbon for her hair and almost everything lost to her, except the will to hold on and not be beaten by what death can do to families and friends.'

I had a foot on the stairs. I must go down and stop this mangling of an old lady's grief. There was a small locked box on the mantelpiece and we all wondered what it held. The old lady was unpinning the glass brooch and had taken out a small key, that was fixed to it. She had opened the box on the chimney piece and there was a large key in it and it could only be the key of the barn. He held it between his fingers.

'It was time somebody told me,' Grandmother said.

'The girl's turned into a pauper for the care she took of me and mine. Loyal Ann! All of them loyal and myself blind to anything but my own selfishness. Thank you Fergus, but don't be in haste. You're welcome to stay awhile. One of these days, I'll get the courage to drive into town in the governess cart by myself. Wait till I'm clear of Cloncon. You have the key now and I'd like you to carry the plan through. Just don't let me see the barn open nor remember that night. If there is nothing, and I think that is likely, leave it all to the rats still and the door safe locked again. I want no part of Glen Leven, unless I'm forced to take it by humanity. Do you hear me? and I thank you.'

She turned to go and then came back again.

'If there's anything left that's of use to Cloncon, then Cloncon is welcome to it. I'll put the matter in your hands to do as you think fit and I'll go by what you say, Fergus Cluny. The idea has come in my head that you're the captain now, the same as you were in the market town, when I hear you defended the lady.'

She cackled at him like a witch and seemed to disappear into thin air and that was that.

We had several secret discussions, but nothing much seemed to be about to happen. Then out of the blue one day, Uncle James announced to us at the table that Gran was going to drive herself with the bay mare into Kilcormac, the market town.

'Alone?'

'Yes, alone. I've just to get the turn-out ready and see that the mare is properly groomed and I'd advise you all to keep your mouths shut.'

We knew she had never driven herself since the day she arrived at the cottage. She had never appeared in the local town. The few times she had come to Derrycreevy had been voyages of adventure and necessity and she had hired a car. She had Aunt Kate help to get her ready and I shall never forget the appearance she made at the top of the stairs. She had unearthed a black tailored coat with a divided skirt, from some old trunk. There was a high white stock at her throat with the glass brooch. She had elegant riding boots that just peeped their toes out from under the lifted skirt. Maybe she had stepped straight down fifty years of *Weldon's Journal*. She had a silk top-hat and a veil that held it in perfection. I had never seen her lovelier. Maybe she had a look about her of a French "aristo" en route for the guillotine. I thought I knew the whole story and if I did not, surely it was written in every inch of the pride of her. Not one of us dared show surprise that she was to go off by herself. I had given Shamus, as Uncle James always called him, a specially good grooming. He had a new-washed silk handkerchief to sit opposite her in the governess cart. I can never describe the way he sat up as proud as Punch. I know we were all proud of her. We saw her as far as the road and watched her drive off out of sight. She showed us how to handle a horse in harness in a governess cart. I wondered if maybe she wept a little, when she was alone.

Then we all went back to Cloncon and we felt ashamed and underhand because of what we had more or less forced on her.

Fergus was in an ill humour and he treated us as crew. It seemed that perhaps he despised us for the position in which we had landed him. He produced the key.

'Here it is then. Much good may it do any one of us!'

Then he thought more of it and went on to tell us his opinion of us. Here was another side of Fergus, the sea-man.

'You're a right pack of fools, every one of you. If you had used your wits, you could have had this door open, by lifting it off its hinges. You could have looked inside and had it on its hinges again. You could have emptied out that stuff years ago and kept it secret. Two strong determined men could have done it any time in the last twenty years. It's my opinion that you've been under some sort of spell of fear of her.'

'You don't know Maw,' said Uncle James.

'Damned key probably won't turn now either,' grumbled Fergus. 'We'll likely have to lift the door off the hinges anyway.'

The key turned in the lock easily enough but the hinges screeched like a banshee keening a death from the Skerry Dhu.

There was a smell that came out to meet us of must and decay. The straw might have been piled high the first night in the light of the hurricane lamps. Almost you could see the carts still and the smugglers from the tax-man, and death just past. You could still sense the haste and the fear and the shock and the total disaster to the whole beautiful House of Glen Leven.

I tried to pull myself together and not take to flights of fancy. It was clear enough what had happened. The barn roof had been the traitor. It had leaked a little and then more and more. The weather had not been shut out. The elements had played havoc with what was the pick of the furniture of an old house. There was fungus and dry rot and wood worm and rats and moth and rust and total destruction. I looked at a tallboy that held blankets and linen and it was filigreed with old hatching of grubs, that had come to nothing. It had crumbled in on its own structure I could only think of Rider Haggard's *She*, the immortal *She*, who must be obeyed.

The furniture was a write-off. More than that. It was a danger to any house that gave it shelter. The barn had caught the infection. There was fungus that sprouted on the roof beams . . . and ran up the walls, great evil-looking mushrooms like gargoyles.

A silence had fallen and somehow that night was back again when they had all made what was probably their last frantic effort to save Maw. They were beyond speech with the disappointment and the tragedy of it, but Fergus was flint.

'This barn is dynamite,' he said. 'It will bring down the cottage and every building in the place. This treasure house of yours could make sawdust of Cloncon. We haven't much time to do it, but every bit of the barn and its contents must be burnt and buried at once and we'll want some of your oil, Ann, to get it done in time. We've spied into a great secret tragedy. It's done us no good, except maybe to prevent the end of Cloncon, but not the beginning.'

Fergus was angry with us. He had been angry from the start, but we had not read him rightly. He turned back to us.

'You're not to blame,' he said to the sad little group we were. 'Don't go pinning guilt on yourselves. Haven't you thought it through even yet? Ann, don't you understand now? It was Angus Hamilton's wife let it all go. She put her own sorrow first. She was so hurt that she lashed out in pain, didn't care who went to the wall. Maybe it was her right to let her own children suffer, but I don't think so. She didn't want to see it any more, so she left it to rot. I imagine she might have looked through the window a time or two and seen Himself dead on the hurdle in his pink coat, and the world finished. She had no gratitude to any one of you that tried to save the wreck. Did she ever try to thank anybody? Did she never mention that Miss Kate as a child had caught the horse and saved Hamilton's body being dragged half across the county?'

Fergus had taken a hay fork and was furiously lifting the straw aside. The furniture was a pile of kindling. I went wandering off with an order to bring buckets of oil up to the back field.

'We've got to get this barn and all its contents out there and send it up.'

'There isn't time,' said Uncle James. 'It'll have to go up where it stands. The wind is blowing off the garden. It won't carry the flames to the house. We'll watch it.'

It was agreed that the barn had the power to destroy the house and Gran would have to face up to maybe a conflagration when she got back. One of us would walk out to meet her and prepare her for the disappearance of what had been a kind of awful monument.

Right at the bottom of all the corruption, we found the remains of a beautiful desk. It halted Fergus in his tracks. There was such a desk in Gorse Hill House and he knew it of old. It had been his father's and it was his now, shining with bees' wax.

'There was a secret drawer in that type of desk,' He said.

'For God's sake, Bessie, get on with it,' Uncle James cried. 'The cat's away and the mice are having a hell of a time of it. The same cat can turn home, halfway to Kilcormac and arrive here in our midst. We've got to have it all tidied up before she has time to come home.'

'I know this sort of desk well,' Fergus said and squatted down and riffled through small drawers of exquisite craftsmanship. He slid his fingers through the small sheets of mahogany that had been shelves and maybe drawers. He came on the front of an angled space and slid his fingers, gently, gently . . . It was away in at the back, that he searched for what he knew must be there . . . an unaccounted-for space and there was nothing to be found.

'It must have been. I know it was. It must have been . . . if it wasn't on the other side.'

His left hand was feeling carefully now, turning over the small slats of wood and the metal door knobs.

'Yes, there's something left still, wrapped . . .'

With exquisite care, as if it might come to pieces in his hands, he disinterred something that had held out against the years. It was dusty and black green, oiled silk.

'That should have saved it.'

It was double wrapped, we saw as he brought it out to the light. On the sill of the barn window, he opened it and we stood around in a semi-circle and watched him.

'Miss Hamilton,' he said to Aunt Bessie. 'It seems your right to read it. I imagine that your mother might throw it in the range, especially when she sees what we're going to do to the barn.'

He gave a small smile to show me that he was still the same gentle Fergus I loved, and not some conquering naval hero, that might terrify me out of my wits.

Aunt Bessie lifted it layer from layer with gentleness. The oil silk wrapping, the envelope that was discoloured by time.

'God's sake, Bessie, get on with it,' Uncle James muttered. 'The old lady will be back on us before we've even fired the barn.'

The envelope was best parchment addressed in an ornate hand.

Mrs. Constance Peppard Hamilton.

Fergus did not have Aunt Bessie's delicacy, for she sat and looked at the letter for so long that he took it from her and opened it, took out a sheet of writing paper engraved Strawberry Hill, dated a long time ago. With no hesitation, he read it all out to us and I thought there might be hell to pay when the cat came home. It was from her father for the Heiress of Strawberry Hill.

My dearest Constance,

'In case I should be gone and still no friendship between Hamilton and me, and you have been loyal to him as a wife should be, my mind is uneasy. There is no happiness and you and I are of a kind . . . proud and stubborn . . . maybe two mules.

Who am I to judge Hamilton, for surely that's God's prerogative? Yet if I was right, you may one day find it out and know need and regret, I cast about in my mind what to do. I see the way you ride to hounds these days and no care if you break your neck. Maybe it's as well he's turned you to breeding, for you seem set on killing yourself. Some poet said "youth at the prow and pleasure at the helm", but I'm not one for poetry. I just do not want to see you in poverty and degradation. You're the only person that ever has mattered to me. I've been too proud to seek you in Glen Leven, and I have waited in vain for you to come to me, and you too proud to come.

So I consulted the bankers and they say gold is safe, so I put a bag of gold in a strong box in the Bank of Ireland. I locked a great many sovereigns away and all that remains in evidence is the key of it. The key is yours with this . . . a crock of gold. You take this key to Dublin and they will give you the gold, but maybe I want to give you something of greater value and that is to tell you that I never lost the love I had for you. You were scornful and independent, but so was I. I thought I was clever to leave you my writing desk in my will and nothing else. I wondered if you would recall the secret compartment. Does it seem a very long time ago, when I had to leave your Saturday sixpence in it? You would come riding up the avenue and tie the Shetland to the mounting block fence. Constance, my darling! If only we could turn back time, maybe it would not flow away in bitterness a second time.'

Affectionately yours . . . Peppard.

We were all stunned into silence, but Fergus was putting the oiled silk package together again. The small key rattled against the sill of the barn and he put it in his pocket and the envelope of oiled silk too.

'It only remains to contact the Bank of Ireland. There's a

fortune waiting for the old lady. She'll have to get a solicitor to deal with it. It's foolproof. It seems that Cloncon is at an end of its penury. Strange how there was treasure here after all.'

I found myself chattering like a monkey.

'It means that that we can afford all the things we wanted. We can have the electricity laid on as soon as it comes . . . the pylons. We can get power to pump the water. We'll not have to fetch oil any more. We can have proper sewerage. We can advance from the middle ages to modern living. I can get away from here now and can go home to Derrycreevy and get Annie and Sarah back and we can start on Derrycreevy at last . . .'

Fergus had his arm about me.

'Best get the barn burnt first, and it strikes me that there's one priority. We've got to prevent the Czarina's heart being broken when she reads that letter.'

We were all uneasy about the impact the letter might have on her. Fergus offered to walk out along the road to meet her coming home, tell her all that had happened.

'Get rid of the bonfire before we get back. Mrs. Hamilton had a sad end to her marriage and a sad end to her life, it seems if some miracle hasn't happened now and that's not impossible. She must be allowed to mourn and this is one time she will be very sad. She will see only the ashes of the treasure of Glen Leven.'

I shook my head at him

'Maybe I've drawn the short straw this time, Fergus. That letter could finish her, if you read the implications into it, so it holds, I'm the one to explain it to her. I think I can do it too and maybe it's my privilege.'

I turned and ran like a jack rabbit. I did not want to see the match struck and the flames creeping, the timbers catching, catching easily, for Fergus would have been generous with the oil. The straw would frizzle and then the matchwood kindling of all that was left of Glen Leven, all that lovely furniture come to corruption. It was such tragedy and waste and sorrow. I did not wait for permission to go and meet the old lady. I went. I vaulted over the post and rails of the front entrance and was off across the first field and through the gap, then on to the entrance to the farm and the bone-dry mud. I knew how to vault a gate, so I was soon over the hurdle and out in the lane and the surface of it was dried mud and there was no stopping me. I paused at the main road and turned left towards Kilcormac. Behind me there was a spiral of smoke and I knew it had started. Thoughts were rocketing round my brain. Indeed we had found treasure, but the letter was strange. Gran had broken with her father, but it was obvious that it had been one of these ridiculous fights, between two obstinate proud people. I tried to straighten out what had happened and thought it was the usual stuff of family feuds. Gran had loved Hamilton and she had stuck to him and her father had been left with an empty hearth and bags of sovereigns and I thought that gold pieces were no equal to an array of fine grandchildren, who would have run in and out of Strawberry Hill and tormented the life out of Peppard. How he must have wanted them . . . Bessie and Kate and James and John and Stuart and Mother . . . all lost to him. I was glad I had not seen the firing of the barn. At least we had money now, at least Gran would have it. It must be a formidable sum. Sovereigns were valuable these days. It seemed that we had credit to buy what was life-saving for Cloncon.

I knew my grandmother. She was as likely to throw the gold into the deepest bog hole she could find and say 'To hell with Strawberry Hill. I want none of it . . .'

I walked along the country road and listened out for the clip-clop of the mare's hooves on her way coming home. I reached Tinna Cross after the three-mile walk and still no sign of the governess cart. I was getting anxious about her. She was a very old lady and really we should not have let her go alone. Behind me the pillar of smoke still rose to the sky, but by now, it might be past its worst . . . the conflagration. I pictured the shower of blazing sparks and the smell of the oil, and how the rafters would crash one after another. The oiled silk package was a weight in my pocket and I had buttoned it securely. What would she think of the letter from her father? Would it seem a long time ago to her when she had come in every "payday" as a small child . . . tethered her Shetland pony to the fence and gone into the study at Strawberry Hill to collect her Saturday pennies from papa's secret drawer? She had never been reconciled with her father, not after so many years. God only knew what his letter might do to her. It might smash what happiness she had, if she had any at all.

It was late enough in the afternoon when I heard the trotting hooves. I stood and waited for her and she came and the dog sitting as proud as Punch still. He leaped out of the trap and came running to meet me, licked my face and shattered the quiet with his barking. I picked him up in my arms and raised my hand to her and she swirled the whip along the mare's back and drove up to where I stood and there was still a flourish to her and the mare stepping smartly.

I had an apple in my pocket and the crop-crunch of the mare's teeth against my flattened palm was a welcome sound.

'It was kind of you to walk so far to meet me.'

I went round to the back of the trap and put the dog back on the seat, and got in behind him.

'Maybe, it's very good news for you I have,' I said.

'Have you? you indeed? I can't see that much good can come out of Cloncon barn.'

I took out the oil-wrapped package and set it on the seat in front of her. She let the mare crop at the long grass on the verge and looked at the package as if it were a snake.

'There was nothing of Glen Leven to find in the barn, Gran. The years had taken it all, only this one thing. I think it's very important. The Glen Leven furniture was all gone to dust. The desk was in pieces too, past being regenerated. It

had been left in the Strawberry Hill will . . . left to you, the
only thing . . . and it had been packed away with the other
stuff in the barn and never looked at . . .'

I watched the small cloud of smoke that was all that was
left of the great fire. She made no effort to touch the package.

'It had been a desk with a secret compartment, that you
knew of. Fergus knew the sort of desk. He searched the
remains and he found that package with the letter. We read
it and you'll be angry about that.'

'Pappa left me his desk in the will and that was all. Pappa
and Angus Hamilton had fallen out about my marriage
settlement. Pappa said at the time that he would rather put a
wreath on my grave. There was no sense in them, never was
sense in anything.'

She smiled at me.

'And did Fergus find a sixpence in the secret drawer?'

She could not hide the pain from her face and I took the
package, opened it, lifted out the envelope and put in her lap.

She did not touch it and after a bit I opened the envelope
and put the letter in her hand to read.

She read the ornate writing slowly once and then again,
read the legal document.

I expected her to weep, but nobody could call it weeping.
A slow glycerine tear ran down one cheek and then the other
and she was impatient with tears.

'So he left me a fortune and it's not important any more,'
she said.

'Of course, it's important,' I said sharply. 'Have you
thought what gold is worth today compared with then? Have
you thought that this bag of sovereigns can harness
electricity to Cloncon? The pylons are almost within reach.
You can banish the oil and the water tank on the roof. You
can strangle the infernal pump. You can hire help on the
farm. You can get drains. You can buy pedigree stock. You
could have central heating if you wanted it . . . and
comfortable chairs. You needn't worry yourself silly when

the bills come in. You've not to wonder how to meet the rates
nor have you to make Uncle James get up at half five and
milk the cows. Uncle James can have his breakfast in bed if
he pleases, brought up by a pretty girl in a nylon overall.'

'Can he indeed.' she demanded. 'You paint a pretty
picture.'

'Yet maybe he was the best of them all, Madame,' I said.
'He never deserted you, when they all deserted you and fled
. . . or almost all. He's not Caliban and he's not Tony
Lumpkin and always you do him ill-justice.'

'Hoity-toity,' she said. 'But the wonder was that Pappa
was reconciled to me. He never put me out of his heart . . .
and I had been wrong. I know it now. He had the right of it.
Poor Pappa!'

She said no more, just packed the letter away in her
reticule, but she read it again first. Maybe she intended to sit
there for ever, so at last I appealed to her.

'And I can go home to Derrycreevy, Gran? Soon I can go?
I've collected so many certificates of education. I have them
in a little box every last one of them. If I choose, I can go to
university now, but I'm sick for home, like Ruth was. I think
I'll die if I don't go home . . . if I don't rescue Annie and
Sarah out of the Convent. I want to go home, then when I go
home, maybe I'll not achieve all I meant to achieve, but it's
time I went. It's time I remembered Derrycreevy and what's
to be done there. I must get the house on its feet again. I
wanted to get a medical degree, but my certificates have all
come up for the arts and no sciences. I could go to the
university, but my degrees would not work out for medicine.
It would take too long and I'm no good at all. I can get the
house right with hard work. Annie and Sarah would be home
again. I pray to St. Luke to send me a doctor for the practice
and it's mighty unfair on the new doctor . . .'

I had let myself get too emotionally involved and she was
severe enough with me.

'Never pray for the impossible, Ann,' she said. 'Don't be

like the story of the Monkey's Paw, by W. W. Jacobs. No doubt you know it. The monkey put his paw in the bottle and he filled it too full . . . never could get that paw free again, and that was the end of him.'

She laughed at me and she seemed in high good humour against my despair.

'But I must go home to Derrycreevy, Grandmother.'

'Of course, you must, child. Maybe you think I've been sitting here sad, but you're wrong. I think I was seeing you for the first time and remembering that maybe I was just the same when I was your age.'

She smiled at me and put out a hand on mine.

'I can't let you go and not tell you the full story, for you didn't know it . . . not the way it was. You didn't see it, no more than my children did. They actually lived it and still didn't see it, but you must be told.'

'I want to go home,' I wailed like a child and she comforted me like a child and said I should go home soon.

'And thank you, Ann. Cloncon has "gone up the ladder and down the wall". In two years we've inched back to comfort and maybe civilisation. Now you present me with my fortune today and we can make a further start. If I had possessed a heart like you, child, I'd never have lost Glen Leven, but I didn't want it. That surprises you, but I said, I'd tell you the truth.'

She sat there and wondered how to tell me whatever she wanted to tell me and at last she had it.

'Hamilton could have saved Glen Leven, but he was given no second chance. If he had turned and tried the double bank again, he might have made it, but he was killed outright and poor Kate trying to catch his horse. God knows I've learnt my lesson in Cloncon . . . how hard it is to make a penny piece . . . and all that stuff in the barn and I wouldn't touch it. Do you know why? Maybe you'll not believe it. I hated Glen Leven . . . hated Angus Hamilton and now the secret's out! Father was right about Hamilton. I was a spoilt miss and I thought he was like Young Lochinvar. He eloped with me at the church gates, when I was to wed an earl, that was Father's choice for me. I lived a lie all my married life . . . hated it. I didn't know what marriage was. My father had picked a good match for me, but I thought I could pick my own love and I never knew what love was, from first to last.

'Afterwards, when I saw marriages like your father and mother, I knew I had missed out on life. Maybe I was spoilt in the upbringing when I was the queen of Strawberry Hill. I even told lies about the green brooch . . . said Angus gave it to me for James's birth. That was a lie. I never wanted the marriage bed. I never wanted children. Life was all gaiety and entertaining and castles in the air . . . no reality about it, but I know what's real now. This glass brooch came from Strawberry Hill, from my father.'

She stopped up short and laughed and changed her mind.

'Maybe it came out of one of Harrod's crackers. It was my good luck piece. I'll never be parted from it . . . I recall how Father laughed when I called it the glass brooch.'

I took in some of what she said and could not believe it all. I gathered that she had not understood marriage nor given a thought to the reality of living. It was common enough, that sort of ignorance in those old days. She had had so many children that she did not know what to do. She had hated them and hated him and resented it all. She had dreaded the time when she had to go to bed with him. She had never found love and tenderness and missed love and missed living.

'I was so happy as a little girl,' she said. 'I didn't want to grow up, but Hamilton soon forced me to grow up. I was free when he was dead. God forgive me! I was free, but I had to put on mourning. I wanted no more to do with Glen Leven. We were bankrupt anyway and I wanted to run and never stop running. No matter where I've ended up I knew it could not be worse than legalised rape every night and a child born every year, so that if I had not a babe at the breast, I was with child.'

Suddenly she was horrified at the way she had poured out the secret of her life. She apologised quietly for speaking of such a matter to a young girl. I must be horrified at her, but I shook my head and told her that times had changed.

'Maybe it was better to be innocent,' I said. 'Now it's all different and maybe evil. A boy can say to a girl at school, that if she doesn't have sex, she's only a kid, and a child is lost to know which is the right way. I was lucky to find Fergus, for he's the same as I am. He thinks that maybe he's for me and I'm for him. With good fortune, that's how it will be. It's not necessary for us to experiment to see what's right. We know what's right and we're maybe two souls on one body now. I'm for him and he's for me. I want nobody else.'

I thought it strange that Gran was another ladybird, whose children had been scattered to the ends of the world. Glen Leven's children had been scattered like sheep and his grandchildren. Bo-Peep could never gather up all her flocks now. It had all been such a cruelty of waste.

'Were all Rohan's children like you, Ann? I never did meet another the same as Ann of Derrycreevy. If the others were the same, it's no wonder God took them back to himself. I've always thought that you were left alive to put right a wrong and I think you'll do it . . . but then I'm a fanciful foolish old woman. To think that there was something left outstanding, that had to be put right. I mean the folly of Glen Leven and the Peppards.'

'Best get back to Cloncon,' I whispered. 'It will be dark soon.'

I tucked the rug about her and offered to drive, but she was far too independent for that. A mile along, we met Uncle James, riding the cob bareback, a canter on the grass verge. he was laughing in the way he had, just because he could not abide sad faces.

'Thank the Lord ye're all in one piece. Back at the house,

they have you both dead and buried with the night coming down and no sign of either one of you ever again.' He wheeled the cob to ride alongside Maw, maybe read anger on her face.

'I was wondering why the chicken crossed the road,' he grinned. 'I just thought of an answer to it. It seems that she saw the sign that there was a fifty shilling fine for "fowling" the pavement. She got off the path smartish.'

Maw slashed out across his shoulders with the whip and I thought how she wronged him.

'Caliban,' she screeched. 'Riding out all these miles, just to pretend you care whether we're dead or alive. Just to produce a specimen of your vulgar jokes too, and your boots reek of the stables. Go on and take yourself home and wash at the pump before you appear at table.'

He took the fence by the road in a clean leap and then back again. His ringing laugh frightened the rooks that were coming in to land in the elm trees.

'It's my wellingtons, Maw. Maybe it's my feet, as the centipede said. Forgive my feet. That was the centipede, wasn't it? There was so many of them they took too long to wash.'

I had started to laugh for it was his usual nonsense, but Uncle James turned it off sharp. He appeared at my side suddenly.   'There's been a telegram, Ann. They brought it out from the sub-post office, sent from Mrs. Cluny from Ballyboy. Your Fergus has been recalled from leave, some emergency or another, didn't say. He's got to rejoin his ship at once. He's very fed up about it. They're to stop the main Cork Express at Ballybrophy tomorrow morning and take him aboard, so it's important. Nine hundred hours. It's all fixed.'

His hand rested on my shoulder.

Don't fret, Ann. He'll come back safe again. I thought you were after him as a doctor for Derrycreevy.'

'He's tied to the Navy,' I said. 'He signed on years ago and he can't just walk away. It's his duty. Don't you think I've prayed?'

The old lady looked at me seriously and told me not to forget the Monkey's Paw.

To hell with the monkey's paw, I thought and looked up high into the trees at the cawing rooks, thinking I didn't care.

'Oh, God! Send me a doctor for Derrycreevy,' I prayed in defiance against heaven.

Uncle James was watching me and guessed my thoughts.

'They'll *want* a doctor in Derrycreevy too,' he told me. 'Your man there has had enough of Ireland. He's handed in his notice to the dispensary and he's headed for New Zealand. He had his new bungalow up for sale for what he gave for it and he's aiming to be off in six months. He wants a job that will bring him in coin.'

I clenched my fists in my pockets for the thoughts that rushed my head. Poor mixed up Caliban, who should have been the heir to Glen Leven and maybe to Strawberry Hill too. He took the cob along the road in front of us and he demonstrated the fact that he had taught the cob the rudiments of *haute école*. He moved from one routine to another and the cob went faultlessly, just for the space of time, he went thought the correct paces . . . no saddle and Uncle James like a centaur . . . the cob like a dancer. At the end, he took the leap that maybe only the Lepanzers do and Mary Stewart wrote a book about it and called it *Airs above the Ground*. Just for one moment, the cob leapt into grace and classic beauty. Then Uncle James took off his cap and yelled the war cry of the Southern States as they rose into battle. It was his war cry of glory and I knew it, against all the ills life had dealt him. It tore the closing darkening sky open again. Then he faced the cob at a double bank of gorse and heather. One great powerful leap to the top and a neat change of feet . . . to land at the far side as lightly as thistledown. There was an open field and he went off across it at full gallop. I imagine that his thoughts galloped apace with the cob.

Given a fair chance, he would jump the moon. This very day we had found a new chance for Cloncon. We could see the glow of the burnt-out barn in the distance and I knew that the future of Cloncon must be just as bright.

'So Caliban has dreams, child?' the old lady said. 'Of course he has. Given a chance, he'd not have landed in Cloncon. Life dealt him bad cards, but it wasn't his fault. He never had a trump, but maybe he has one now. You've no idea what your coming to Cloncon has been to every one of us. You have brought a second chance.'

Her thoughts were echoing mine.

'Poor Jamie,' she said, 'Jamie was my baby's name for him. The best of them all.'

And there had been Jamie Rohan and James Cluny . . . a long time ago. Suddenly my eyes filled with tears and I was glad the darkness had come down, as we drove into the front garden at Cloncon and a welcome there for us, and the brightness of the smouldering barn a sign of what the future bore for Cloncon, and a good supper ready for us on the table.

CHAPTER SIX

The Monkey's Paw

It was like Christmas that night and Cloncon kitchen at its best. Aunt Kate and Aunt Bessie were at the door waiting for the lights on the governess cart. James had stabled the cob and was waiting to take the trap. On the long table, the supper was ready to serve. We did not know it, but we had come to a cross-roads in time.

Fergus was due to climb up the high steps to the Cork Express at nine hundred hours next morning. In a few days, Aunt Bessie and I would be off for Derrycreevy in the governess trap. Any moment now, Annie and Sarah would be away from the Convent and home again. Dinny and Michael would be intent on shining the brasses to glory and getting the garden ship-shape. The dust sheets would be whisked off the furniture and a smell of furniture polish overall. Coyle, the butcher, would pick out his best sirloin of beef, so there must be horse radish to dig and scrape, and Sarah's eyes running with tears at the scraping.

It was past the time for Derrycreevy to awaken from slumber. There should be a sparkling of happiness again. It was time Dinny was manning the front steps and the gold watch on his waistcoat. I was so happy just because I knew there was no doctor in Ballyboy or soon there would be no doctor . . . and then . . .

'St. Luke. Please send me a doctor like Rohan. I'll trade my soul for a doctor. Let it all happen again. Rohan from Heaven! Let it all happen and come back to what it used to be.'

It was going to come true for Cloncon. Had not Fergus and Uncle James worked it out over the supper table? It only wanted a connection to the pylons of the Shannon Scheme and we would have power and light and water pumped . . . and maybe hired help and even some pedigree stock for breeding. It was the end of Cloncon's troubles, all in a bag of old gold sovereigns.

If you go to the Dublin Horse Show any day now and if you want to own a moonbeam, you can bid for one of the Cloncon's Arab thoroughbreds, and possess perfection. You can talk with James Hamilton and maybe think he is the happiest man you ever met. You may think there is a story to him and there is. So Cloncon was at the cross roads that night and set for success and happiness.

I was praying for happiness for Fergus, but maybe Fate works in a perverse way.

The next morning I held him tightly, as he kissed me goodbye. Then I watched the Cork Express speed away up the line to Dublin and maybe he was on his way to the Third World, but I did not know it.

'Help me, God. Keep Fergus safe to come home again. Rohan, if you're up there, make it all right for Derrycreevy. Oh, Rohan! Look down and help us find happiness once again, even if yourself is not in it anymore.'

So what happened was my own fault. I was just a small greedy monkey, who dipped a greedy paw into a jar of sweets. Maybe I deserved what I got. It might have been different. Fergus might have become an Admiral.

I know now that he did not. Health, wealth and happiness, I wished for him and I wonder if God was listening to my prayer . . . or St. Luke . . . or Rohan himself. It is for the reader to judge. I know what I think of it now. As a child I can never remember Rohan refuse me anything.

I did not receive the letter that Fergus had left for me in Cloncon, till I came home from driving him in the trap to meet the Express. I was feeling very lonely and it was normal enough. After I had turned the mare loose, I decided to go into the office. It was time to get my gear packed ready for my journey to Derrycreevy. I found the letter from Fergus almost at once. He apologised that he had borrowed, without my permission, the envelope too. He had even used my sealing wax and his own crest on it, the griffon ducally gorged, rampant. He had propped the envelope against a ship in a bottle, that was on the shelf over the fire. Himself had brought it to me from foreign parts.

ANN, ANN, ANN.

Tonight I have been recalled so urgently, that an express train must stop tomorrow, to collect me. Ireland is such a pleasant place where time is meant for slaves and where things that are important get priority and I thank God that time tables are not omnipotent. To make you smile, when you feel sad, I copy Uncle James and remind you of an old chestnut. It was about the man that landed at Cork from a liner and was very worried about his train connection, and he rushed up to the porter and asked him what time the boat train went.

The porter looked at him from a serene countenance and told him with serenity, 'When ye are all ready, the train will leave sir, and not before. Rest tranquil! This is a civilised country.'

May God hold Uncle James in the hollow of his hands, but this evening I got the recall, sharp and quick and definite. I had not told you but I have been awaiting it. I have come to a point in time and I know why my leave is cancelled. I came home, on a leash and a mighty short leash too. I find myself inarticulate now but did you not always call me "the dark silent one" and my brothers, the Zebedee twins, rest them in peace, like two Katherine wheels at full glory they were, but no more, or perhaps now in greater glory than ever they knew, but enough of that.

Now tonight, I must put down in writing what maybe I never said. It was my job to hold a family together, maybe two families. A fine job I made of it! You had the same task thrust on you and we were stunned with the impossible tasks we had to face. At any rate, maybe we held the bits together, that were left to our care. I think I have failed to let you know how completely I love you, for what's left of my life.

Now, out of nothing, I find a duty put on me that must be done.

Maybe St. Crispin's day is coming up, but I'll have to be there, at the other side of the earth, and thinking of the cows in Ballyboy, who are wise enough to walk against the one-way traffic on their way out from the milking. They restore me to sanity.

Little Cat. You're due to go back to Derrycreevy soon and it may be hard for a while. I would have liked to have gone with you. I know how to tackle the job, but I am up and away to a task you might not think important to us in a world you could not even imagine.

Listen, Ann! Derrycreevy may be incredibly hard for a time, but there is no turning round and going back for either of us.

I'll be coming home to Ballyboy as soon as I can. I want a fine wedding from Ballyboy church and we'll lay on the matelots with crossed swords. Then we'll decide the future. We both want the House of Derrycreevy to be what it has always been. I have the dream of living happily ever after in an old house by a river, a river where the big fish is king.

I want to come home and stand on the Celtic Carpet and call up the staircase.

'Hear this! Hear this! Cluny is home from sea.' This is my dream of heaven – all I ever want. I love you Ann. I'll love none other. You are an elusive spirit and you've haunted me all my life. Never let me go. Even if it seems that I'm gone. I'll only be out of your sight. I love you so much tonight, I'm like to die of it, because I must leave you alone. Derrycreevy is my happy port, where I creep, back and back again and again. Goodbye and my love to you. God keep you in his care till I come home from sea and find you again, my Ann, my love.

Fergus.

I read the letter over and over and the clouds were coming up the sky, starting at the horizon on a black indigo bar. You could hear thunder rumbling in the distance and I knew a foreboding of fear, which turned my stomach to ice.

There was something that Fergus had not dared to tell me. Maybe there was a duplicate moment way back in time, when I had stood at the ticket box of the roller-coaster. It was all going to happen again? I knew it must be all imagination. How could it all happen again? This was only an autumnal thunderstorm. Soon it would be on us and then it must pass by.

I was right. It was short and sharp and then the sun was a scatter of diamonds in the grass.

In no time at all, but it seemed long, there we were, Aunt Bessie and I, setting out along the rutty lane on our way home to Derrycreevy. They all walked with us out to the main road and even then, they did not turn back, but went another half mile.

So, goodbye, goodbye, goodbye.

It was no use to linger over farewells. By early evening, we were within exciting reach of Ballyboy.

'Let's see whom we meet first, that we know,' suggested Aunt Bessie. There was another mile and the bridge to cross, that crossed the river further down. Then came Gallows Hill and the high limestone wall of our estate. My heart was beating fast, but I knew this was no occasion for tears. I found the reins tossed into my hands from Aunt Bessie.

'Drive her in style, Honey. We're coming home.'

The mare knew well where she was. Her black ears were cocked forwards and her shoes rang music. She had been Rohan's mare and doubtless she hoped to see him again. She whinnied as if she called to him and I was daft enough to wonder if he could hear her. I slowed her a little to turn into the gate and there was Michael waiting for us. They were all at the front door, Annie and Sarah come home too. Dinny had never had to quit his guard post and the gold watch was as splendid as ever, so that I saw it through tear-filled eyes. Michael had shut the gates and was haring down the avenue to meet us and perhaps not much coherence in our conversation.

We all set about unharnessing the mare and making much of her. She wanted a fresh drink and a hay rack filled with fragrant sainfoin, a handful of carrots, a few apples, a bowl of chaff and bran and oats. We sat about the stable on manger or rail or upturned bucket and we all spoke without waiting for a reply. It must have sounded a strange jumbled conversation. We were recalled to our senses by the "Eeyore" of the donkey over the paddock gate and we started to laugh. The mare had finished her feed by this and here was her old friend come to see her. As a body, we escorted the mare to the paddock gate and the mare was delighted with the reunion. She behaved in a very girlish manner and kicked up her heels and she and the donkey galloped round a bit and then decided to have a roll and they looked so happy that it was a fitting end to our arrival and time to be coming into the house. There was so much to see, so much to discuss, so much to decide and plan.

Surely it was time we broke our fast, said Sarah. The supper would be on the table as soon as we were ready for it.

Supper was served in the dining room, but in no time at all, we transferred it to the kitchen. The mare was dancing a ballet still in the paddock and we had not even started to talk sensibly. I thought how like a feudal household we were, as we all sat down together. We had emerged from two long hard winters and now their eyes were lifted to me and the head of the table. They wanted news, and they hoped for glad news.

I told them about Cloncon and they were very glad, but their hearts were with Derrycreevy and I knew it. At last I came to it, but slowly enough.

'I passed all the exams,' I said. 'You know that I can go to Trinity College now, if I want.'

'Trinity College,' they said, as if I had said I was going to gaol.

I put it off a bit.

'We've got to get something worked out. At least we're together again and you all waited for me. Is the big fish still in the river? Of course he is. Who dare catch him in the town of Ballyboy?'

'I got the wrong exams,' I confessed. 'I passed arts when I should have passed science. It would not be a medical career

I'd have in Trinity. I'd just be well educated and that might not run the estate.'

They should not have been so pleased about it. If it meant that I was to stay at home, that was O.K. by everybody.

We were no experts in careers.

Almost at once, the suggestions were on the agenda. We could choose so many careers for Derrycreevy.

We could breed pigs.

We could sell dairy produce, butter and eggs and milk. We could run beef cattle like they did at Cloncon.

I contradicted.

'No, we must get a new doctor for Derrycreevy. If I can't do it, we must find a doctor who can. Isn't the old dispensary waiting lonely for Himself? We want somebody like Rohan was.'

They pressed it on me that the "new doctor" was off to New Zealand at any moment and there was no time to waste. Rohan's practice was just ticking over and every person in Ballyboy wanting him back again. But he could never come back.

I sank in a feeling of helplessness. Even if I had had science, it would have taken me six years before I was ready for the old dispensary. It was impossible. I drowned in my feeling of failure . . . complete and utter. It had not worked out.

'I believe our new doctor is away soon,' said Annie, and went on. 'Oh, ma'am, I forgot to tell you in the excitement, that Mr. McCarthy is calling to see you tomorrow at ten sharp. He has very important news for you and he says you're to make no decisions till he's seen you, because something terrible important has happened. You're not to worry because it's good news.'

We had an evening like Christmas. I woke the next day with no firm decisions made and remembered.

Desmond McCarthy, ten o-clock sharp, and all the fear came rushing into my soul again. I lay in the master bedroom. For some reason, they had allotted it to me. Here was a room I had known well. I did not remember the shadows that inhabited it. Here we had been born, all we children. Here I had come to see the "new baby", Jamie and Meg and then little Alice.

'But it doesn't matter whether they are boys or girls,' I had said. 'They're just babies now.'

The night had been uneasy with old dreams. It was here that Mother had died. I thought of Fergus and wondered if he was in the third world, maybe in danger of his life. I went out early on and watched for the big trout in the river, but he was not there. Desmond McCarthy and his legal papers were in the dining room. I wondered if he recognised me. I was dressed as a lady in a black formal suit, as befitted the occasion.

Aunt Bessie had let the suit down and out between night and morning. I tucked a carnation into my buttonhole, for Dinny had brought it in specially for me and I did not want to seem ungrateful.

So there Desmond was on the stroke of ten and I went in to meet him and he looking at me, as if I was a stranger. He took my hands in his and held them out from my sides.

'You've grown up, Ann. I'd not have recognised you. I'd have passed you in the street. Rohan will never be dead while you live and breathe. It's uncanny. Yet I remember the Strawberry Hill Heiress and her portrait. You're the spit of her all over again too . . . in your eyes and the set of your jaw, and maybe arrogance too.'

He smiled at me and asked where I had found all the arrogance in my sackcloth and ashes.

'The portrait in Cloncon sitting room?' I said. 'I cleaned it up a bit. I wish I had a tenth of the beauty the Strawberry Hill Heiress possessed, or even a hundredth part.'

His business was confidential. He did not want Aunt Bessie to hear our discussion, though I asked if she might sit in on it.

'Once I tell you what I have to say, you can disclose the facts to any of them, but first it's for your own ears only.'

We were seated at the dining room and Annie had left the decanter of sherry and a silver dish of cheese straws.

'Have you read *Great Expectations* by Charles Dickens?' Desmond asked me and I nodded my head and overflowed his sherry and mopped it up with my handkerchief.

'They tell me you've got your education lined up but not in the sciences. It's no matter . . . no matter at all. You're not dependent on it now.'

'I can't go for medicine, Desmond. I'm a square peg and I'm supposed to be round.'

'Stop larking about,' he said, and I was no longer the Mistress of Derrycreevy, just the girl he remembered from a hundred years ago.

'All right then, you remember Satis House and the Anonymous Benefactor and all the rest of it. It seems that you've got an anonymous benefactor too. You've come into a fortune.'

I wondered if Desmond had gone off his head, but it seemed he had done no such thing. He knew very little of the details of the affair, but a firm from Dublin was dealing with it. Messrs. Longman, Longman, Longman, Jones and Longman, Solicitors. 'Mr. Jones is in charge of your portfolio.'

'Oh?' I said. 'But Desmond, you know that my pockets are inside out. Well you know every detail of that.'

'Not so,' he said. 'I just told you. You're Pip in *Great Expectations,* only I don't think you'll be expected to play with Estella.'

He was very patient with me and we straightened it out at last. Somebody had come forward to provide for me, but he or she would not reveal his or her identity. If I tried to find out, the whole endowment would *become null and void.* There seemed no sense in it, but of course, I knew who it was. It was the old lady of Cloncon. She had inherited the bag of golden sovereigns and she had decided that I must have help.

We waded on through discussion, Desmond and I, and I told him about the find in the secret desk in the barn, but he laughed me out of court.

'Mrs. Hamilton has come into some money. I accept that, and it will set Cloncon up, if they go carefully. This inheritance of yours is something else again. It's a great fortune, many times over what she could have afforded to give you. You can rule out the Czarina for a start. I advise you not to go searching. If you find out who left you the bequest, it will vanish. I thought I made this very clear indeed to you. You must not pry.'

'So it's all a joke?' I said and he opened his briefcase and took out a wad of notes. He had them all arranged and they were brand new. He put them out in five piles of one hundred pounds on the polished mahogany and instantly they reflected themselves double in the shine, so that the whole thing took on the aura of a fantasy.

'You'll want some ready money to be going on with,' he said as casually as he always was about finance, when I could never get matters straight.

'But there is no possible person,' I started and he frowned at me.

'Oh, but indeed there is. Accept it and don't worry yourself about it. I'm not supposed to encourage you to speculate on who has taken on your guardianship. I'd advise you to cast your mind back to all the children of Angus Hamilton. They emigrated and there were many of them. What's to stop one of them ending up childless and alone and maybe a fortune in sheep or whatever and he finds he has a grandchild, who has maybe proved herself? Now don't even think of that, I don't want to be the one to smash anybody's dream of making a fine lady. You'll know it in time. Just for now accept it. Sign this receipt for five hundred pounds to be going on with. Advise me when you want more and leave it to me to open an account for you. I'll appoint myself as your solicitor. You're such a trusting child that I regret I'm not a confidence trickster. It would be like taking a Mars bar off a two-year-old.'

'Strawberry Hill and Glen Leven,' I murmured. 'They threw their money about with no care in the world. It must be mixed up some way with that whole dynasty.'

'Don't open Bluebeard's door. You'll get the chop, Little Cat.'

He was very serious suddenly and he told me this reward was a thing I had deserved. He had watched me live through hell and I had come out unsinged. Desmond was a tried friend and we were very casual with each other. Quickly he told me the details of it. I must stop worrying about the maintenance of Derrycreevy. For the moment, I had a generous allowance and on the death of the anonymous benefactor, I was to be the residuary legatee, of a great deal of money.

'You need never worry about expenses any more,' he said. 'It's my guess this guy is from Australia and he doesn't want to get cluttered up with relations. He's a loner. Let him rest.'

'But I owe so much,' I wailed and he said he did not see what.

'I owe Aunt Bessie and Annie and Sarah and Dinny and Michael . . .'

'Maybe you repaid them. I don't know.'

'I could never repay them. I'll spend the rest of my life at it,' I said.

'Spare me the details,' Desmond smiled and slid the notes across the shining surface of the table. 'Just let me see you put Derrycreevy back where it was. It should be child's play now. All you want is a doctor and the position is advertised in the B.M.J. this week. All you want is a lusty young man, that likes the idea of a salmon river . . . unmarried of course and on the look out for a wife. It's all waiting for the right man.

'Yuck!' I said in disgust. 'Is it? Is it indeed? I'm going to marry Fergus Cluny and you show poor taste to make such a comment.'

It did no good for he was as incorrigible as ever.

'It's as good as done, Ann. Can't you see it?'

'Fergus will never come to Derrycreevy as doctor,' I explained. 'He's tied up with the Navy since way back to Nelson. God! You know that.'

"Yet was it poor little Jamie Cluny who bought the sheep's eye at Coyle's, the butchers, all that time ago, because he wanted to be like Rohan. Doesn't life break your heart with the turns it takes?"

He smiled at me and bent and kissed my cheek.

'Rest tranquil, Little Cat. It will all come right. Just give it time. Don't tell Fergus about the bequest. Tell Sarah and Annie and Michael and Dinny and maybe Aunt Bessie that you've won the Sweep. It's simpler than the other, but it will come to the correct and given time. The mills of God grind slowly, but they grind exceeding small. It's always the same thing . . .'

INTERLUDE

A night between two days

It was a coast somewhere in tropical Africa and the full moon, low on the horizon. Maybe it was the White Man's Grave . . . hot enough for it at any rate. The Surgeon Lieutenant was as silent as he always was, as he watched the shore for the signal. His medical kit was in a pack on his back and he knew he would likely need it. The people on shore were supposed to show a light. It had been explained to the Convent Mission. The R.N. craft was there to take off children from the British Embassy, important children – but then were not all children important?

The nuns were too old for the trek through the jungle, but nuns had a carelessness about their own lives. There was a novice, who knew the path well and possessed youth. Gladly she had agreed to accompany the children. She had the intelligence to carry the torch and to use it carefully.

Dot . . . dot . . . dot . . . dash . . . dash . . . dash . . . dot . . . dot . . . dot . . .

Then one more time.

Dot . . . dot . . . dot . . . dash . . . dash . . . dash . . .

Or was it the other way?

What did it matter? One R.N. issue torch would be a lighthouse to alert the whole jungle and call in the mosquitoes and worse than the mosquitoes . . . ones who watched.

Here it came now . . . a single brilliant flash and no more. Then it came again, just one other anonymous bright light. There was a burst of gun fire in the jungle dark. The country was free at last but not likely to be free for long. The forest area was occupied by khaki clad guerrillas. The men in the boat moved off silently and after a while, the sand of the shore was gritty against their hull.

It was a small incident in a small vicious war, of really no importance whatever. It was easy enough to come ashore. Suddenly there was a clustering of little children about them and excited hands reaching for them – monkey chattering with no heed for silence. They all spoke at once.

'Sister Thérèse broke her ankle . . . can't walk any more. She said we were to go on alone. She showed us a star. We must make for it and there was a path clear enough to see. When we meet the edge of the sea, we must flash the torch, once twice, many times, but not too much. S.O.S. morse. The bad soldiers are all about. They will shoot us. We dropped the torch, not the torch the Reverend Mother gave us, but the super navy torch. Sister Thérèse broke it when she fell. It was Jamie that had the auxiliary torch to flash.

'I'm Jamie,' said the voice.

'Just one more light,' Fergus whispered.

A struck match shaded by the Surgeon Lieut's hand and indeed it seemed another Jamie, aged about ten, with red hair.

'I laid a trail of paper chase. It would lead back to Sister Thérèse. She will be killed by the bad men in the jungle. Somebody must go back to her to carry her out.'

Fergus knew maybe he had drawn the short straw one more time. He took the torch from Jamie's hand and told him not to worry . . . just to go with the sailors.

'But your orders, sir? muttered one of the men.

'Blast my orders. There's a bit of parchment I got one time at a Royal College. I'll try to fetch the girl. Come back for me, but don't wait long. The girl has no chance alone, but they won't touch the Convent itself. I'll carry her out.'

He tousled "Jamie's" red hair.

'It's only a paper chase, Jamie. Do you know I once had two brothers like you?'

It was meant to happen so. He knew it was fate. He found the way easily enough, for it was well trodden and the paper confetti shone white. Yet it seemed a long time till he found the young girl, curled up under a tree and tears wet on her black face. He had the right kit too . . . an inflatable splint for a Pott's fracture, in darkest Africa. Thank God she was so small, but slung across his shoulder, she multiplied her weight. it was a long haul back to the sea. The trees were listening to the pad of his feet and his heavy breathing. The whole forest was a whisper for the listening. Once she gave a small whimper of pain and then no more, only 'I'm sorry, Master.'

Then came the glint of the sea and the boat waiting again, inshore, silent.

'Take her gently. She's got an ankle fracture-splint in. We're O.K. now.'

The children would be safe on the ship . . . embassy children, a chap and a lassie and two little orphans the nuns had collected, a prince of Israel . . . an Arab child, but Jamie was Scots. The Scots were scattered round the third world like flung seed. One of the matelots was saying that Jamie's father owned the whole of the top left-hand side of Scotland, but he was not a stuck-up man It seemed that Jamie's father wore leather patches on his elbows.

Fergus had laid the girl in the boat and had his foot over the gunwale, when the machine gun opened fire from the trees. There was a great tearing pain in his back and it ran down his right leg like flame from a torch. He pitched forwards into the well of the boat and the engine fired and they took to the sea smoothly enough. They tried to make Fergus comfortable, laid him straight, put a jersey under his head, threw a great-coat over him. He could not feel the hands that moved his feet, so his spine was gone. His legs were numb, even his hands. Where all his communications gone? In one blow, he had reached old age. A stroke . . . an old man? Surely not?

With the mind of a doctor, he knew his end when he met it. Just one blast of pain and then no more. It wasn't too much. It was merciful at the finish, he thought to himself.

There was another burst of shooting and the sea was a phosphorescence of bubbles, that hit the surface. The ship had moved in to pick the launch up. Then hands were hauling him on board. They told him the children were safe below. The little nun was in the sick bay. She was fine. They were all fine. The mission had been successfully accomplished. The ship was away at speed out of the range of machine guns.

Fergus was at the edge of consciousness. Had he just received the replacement for the children on the switch-back roller coaster? He did not know.

'Ladybird, ladybird, fly away home.
Your house is on fire, your children are gone.
All except one and that's little Ann . . .
Ladybird . . .'   Maybe it was a small world.

Derrycreevy was almost the last thought in his head. Ann should be home by now. He wondered if he could crawl to her on his hands and knees – ask her for Rohan's crown of glory from the years gone past. Maybe Cluny could come home from sea, but it did not seem likely. He was the last son of all the Clunys and he would not make it to the hospital ship. Finally, he thought of the salmon river and of the big fish that was king of it, and of Ann, and felt a sorrow. He might have made a paradise of Derrycreevy House. Ann would have made a success of Derrycreevy and she would have made a good wife for a sailor. They would have carried on tradition. Maybe their children would have brought the rocking horse to life again, the old rocking horse with the long eyelashes, and the schoolroom with the big old-fashioned desks. Of course, Ann would marry another man, when she had finished her mourning. It would all go on perfectly well without Fergus Cluny. Derrycreevy would never be anything but a happy house, and there were all the pleasant people. Annie and Sarah and Michael and Dinny. Dinny still called her Miss Baby even now, but she was Ann, his Ann. It was a bitter thing to die, not easy after all . . . not easy . . .

CHAPTER SEVEN

My soul for auction

It was impossible that it should be such a wonderful morning. It was impossible that the day was perfect. Maybe the corn was not as high as an elephant's eye, but there was no doubt at all, that everything was coming my way.

Before he went home, Desmond and I told the good news to a tableau assembled in the dining room. The five hundred pound notes were still collecting interest in the mahogany shine on the table.

They looked at it and it mesmerised them. They all spoke at once.

'But it can't be true?'

'Who was there to leave you all that money?'

'It's not Strawberry Hill. That's gone to the rats and the jackdaws. There's nothing there now, only the wind that blows across the heather . . .'

'And Glen Leven is cut up into small mean tenant farms.'

'Miss Ann, well you know the way we're hanging on here by the skin of our teeth. Mrs. Cluny has been fighting a battle against the money that Gorse Hill must have for rates and taxes. Her ladyship over at Cloncon has found prosperity with you and Miss Bessie to help. Ye've set her path on the way to success and Cloncon is saved, just because of what ye did, but there's nobody left. They're all gone. Who could have left such riches?'

'I'm not allowed to speculate,' I said. 'Maybe I said a prayer and had it answered. All I know is that we can get Derrycreevy restored.'

I think I had prayed, but I am not sure. One has not to kneel with bowed head to pray. How often had I prayed for Derrycreevy to be returned to prosperity and now in a snap of a finger it had been done.

'We must get started,' I said.

'I can't see how it will work,' Michael grumbled. 'The new doctor won't want to come here and we haven't Himself any more. We haven't Rohan, who was the heart of it all. Miss Ann hasn't a chance of working for the diplomas in Medicine and Surgery. Lieutenant Cluny is committed for ever to the British Navy and that means he'll never work a country practice in Ballyboy. It's likely that he will end up an Admiral, but what good is that going to do to Rohan's kingdom?'

Aunt Bessie looked at him severely and told him that I would be married to Fergus and live happily ever after, but none of them seemed satisfied with that. Maybe I was greedy like the little monkey.

''Mr. Fergus has lost his brothers. He's the only son left. He can't be unfaithful to his family and throw the Navy aside. He would never be happy as a country doctor in Ballyboy. It would never work out,' Annie said.

My mind was a baulky horse at a jump. It was not necessary to join one's hands palm to palm. Maybe I offered my soul silently. 'Let things work out.' I sent an urgent signal to heaven. I felt my spine tingle as I offered my soul. It was all tied up with good or evil . . . God or the devil. I spoke but there was no sound, just thoughts that were so earnest that they lifted the small hairs on the nape of my neck.

There was no limit to what I was willing to offer . . .

'I'd sell my soul to have Fergus come home to me and be happy . . . to settle in Rohan's kingdom and have his happiness, Rohan's happiness all over again . . . to mind Rohan's sheep. Please! Please! Please! I'd gladly die for it, if it came to that . . . and after death, my soul for auction.'

It was surely an urgent prayer flung at God's feet.

Few prayers have been answered so quickly. It was only a week before the phone rang.

In the meantime, maybe we had been hysterical with activity. The whole town was electric with it and I had tried to keep it secret at first. Miss Ann was an heiress like the Heiress of Strawberry Hill. My credit was unlimited. I like to think that Rohan had some credit too in Ballyboy and that it was not the thought of money to be made, that turned the place into a beehive.

Hoctor's, the contractor's, had the ladders up on the roof in a day or two. Fayle's had rolls of wallpaper down from Dublin. There were painters notified and ready to move in. There was a stack of catalogues of modern kitchens and eye-level ovens. I had just to choose what I wanted and sign cheques. I had a genie in a bottle in that cheque book. Perhaps I had seven days, when I walked about with a notebook in my pocket and a pencil behind my ear, before it all came tumbling down. It did not actually tumble down. It went on but quietly now . . . and the people walked like they were mourners at a funeral. All the joy was dead in their faces and their voices quiet.

It was the seventh day, when the phone rang and perhaps my answer came. I was in the hall and I picked it up automatically and heard Bridie's voice from the Telephone Exchange. I was to go urgently to Gorse Hill House.

'Fast as you can, Miss Ann. Across the river and over the hill. That's quicker. It's desperate news in a telegram from the British Admiralty. God have pity on you.'

I took to my feet and ran, called something to them in the kitchen that there was trouble in Gorse Hill House. It was Mrs. Cluny. I muttered about a telegram from the Navy and then I scurried down the garden path and over the salmon river, up the hill and down the other side . . . up the green lawns to the french windows. The house still looked the same. There was nobody about. The windows looked immaculate as ever. The blinds were not down. Oh, God! Why should I think of such a thing?

There was nobody in the long sitting room. I went straight up the graceful stairs and into Mamma Cluny's bedroom. There was a sound of weeping. They were all about the bed, all the old retainers. They were destroyed with grief. I saw the telegram on the blue carpet and Mamma Cluny stretched out across her bed, and her old women gathered about her, leaning down to take her hands. She was incoherent with shock, poor Mamma Cluny! She started to weep afresh when she saw I was there. I gathered her into my arms and saw the telegram on the carpet under my eyes . . . typed letters on a pasted strip and they jiggled and danced.

> *REGRET TO INFORM YOU THAT*
> *SURG.LIEUT. CLUNY. F.,*
> *HAS BEEN SERIOUSLY WOUNDED IN*
> *ACTION.*

It had happened at 24 hours on a date that I could not add up and it had been sent from their Lordships of the Admiralty. Further information would be signalled as available.

I would never willingly live the days, when life crawled through time. I lost all track of hours, that did not move at all. There were things that stand up sharply to be remembered, like the day that Bridie came up in the Postman's van to Derrycreevy back door.

She found Sarah, and Sarah had come running for me and Dinny and Michael had appeared and we had all looked at the telegram. Then I must go to Gorse Hill.

> *SURG.LIEUT. CLUNY, F., HAS BEEN FLOWN*
> *OUT SUCCESSFULLY TO INTENSIVE CARE.*
> *CONDITION CRITICAL. INJURY OF SPINAL*
> *COLUMN. INVESTIGATIONS PROCEEDING.*
> *HE HAS PARALYSIS OF LOWER LIMBS AND*
> *TREATMENT IS PLANNED. AWAIT URGENT*
> *SIGNAL*

Ballyboy had always had good neighbour quality. Everybody edged that bit together. They all cared so much. I was Rohan's daughter and Rohan had become a legend . . . his father . . . his grandfather. I can recall going into Oakley's bake house one day, some time in all that lost space and Old Oakley giving me a hot doughnut straight out the cauldron on a little brown plate with a picture of a rabbit on it, as if I were a little girl again. He followed it up with a slice of home-baked ham on the prongs of the carving fork, as if it would comfort my sad heart. Perhaps Bridie from the Post Office became a runner of messages. The whole town watched her as she hunted like a hare to our ever-open door. Maybe she spread the news as she ran.

Finaly officialdom arrived at Gorse Hill House in a Navy staff car with a high-ranking official and a woman driver.

This visit I take the liberty of cutting. Surely it was impossible it was happening again, the roller coaster tragedy? Surely lightning only strikes once? The children came no more to dance in the moonlight . . . not after they had fetched Marmee away. It could not all be starting again, but it had started. God knows how it might end.

Let me try to be impersonal and behave with dignity, when I wanted to grovel on the carpet and keen to the skies.

Fergus had a compound fracture of his vertebrae. The bone had severed the spinal cord. It was not a fatal wound but . . .

There was a long blank in what I remember and then I understood again.

Fergus was in England. They had flown him home to a Spinal Unit. They were going to make a heroic attempt to lift the pressing bone.

Did I understand?

Then it seemed hours later, when I was in Gorse Hill House drawing room and we were pretending to eat little iced cakes and drink China tea. I filled out a strong pink gin for the naval officer and helped the driver and myself to one too, and the Captain looked at me gratefully.

It was a major operation, but it was worth the risk. The alternative was for Fergus to be a complete cripple in a wheel chair. Even if the operation was successful, he would be unfit to serve again in the Navy, but he might make a happy life for himself, after all he was a doctor.

From somewhere deep within myself came the flung spear. *THE MONKEY'S PAW. YOU ASKED FOR IT. YOU'VE GOT IT*.

No. no, no, no, no, no, I denied.

Of course, the Navy would fly Mamma Cluny and myself over to England to the Spinal Unit. We were welcome to stay in the hospital till after the operation and as long as we wished.

I cannot leave this section sterile, but it went on so long that I have no accurate account of hours and days and weeks. It was a bad dream and it had an unreality about it. Soon I might wake up. I wll never forget that small isolated white room with Fergus in an orthopaedic bed, stripped of all luxurious illness. I had forgotten how dark his hair was. He was like a hero in some war film on television. His face was sharp and his eyes very deep and somehow he was not Fergus any more. He had a thing like a gallows over the head of his bed and maybe they meant to hang him from the yard arm. I giggled hysterically at the thought of it and the sister thought I had splendid morale.

His lower limbs covered in a frame, meant to take the weight of the bed-clothes. The cylinder was for oxygen and the blood bottle was for blood. I did not have to ask. I knew he was critically ill. They were going in for a last try. The top surgeon explained it all to us. Fergus was not a chap who would wish to survive with such a paralysis. There was a good chance of his coming through the operation. The chance of recovering the use in his limbs was maybe one in four. He had chosen to take it.

My thoughts were a series of coloured slides, that clicked

and moved on. I was standing at the window of the room, looking out on the parklands of the hospital. Mamma Cluny had had a change of character. She had been the wife of a Captain and she was an old hunter, who heard the hounds baying again. She was the strong one now and I was a novice.

'It's the usual routine, Little Cat. It will all end well.'

My mind changed slides and moved on to the next pictures. There was a polo match going on, on a smooth grass lawn, but such a one as maybe I had never imagined existed. There were no ponies, no keen young riders, only men in wheel chairs, men who charged up and down and played a sort of rough croquet, fell over and were picked up, laughed. The corridors had been inhabited by such young men, most of them happy and smiling. If they were lucky they had a pretty nurse in attendance, but most of them ruefully provided their own engines and this meant they were self-propelled and raced each other on the wide corridors, as if they had no care in the world.

Then suddenly it was time for Fergus to be brought to the theatre and a man who was like a Norfolk farmer spoke to us before the operation. They were all so kind, but one was not supposed to weep and wail for mercy. They were Navy personnel. They knew the risk. They accepted it.

'There's a chance of success, Mrs. Cluny . . . Miss Rohan. We'll lift the pressure and we're doing it as quickly as it could be done. The transport was the tedious thing. He chose to do his heroism in the Third World, a long way away. It will be a great triumph for science, if only we got him out in time.'

We sat in a place called the Solarium and nurses came and went. Then after a long time, the Norfolk farmer was back and I thought he might open his mouth and tell us that Fergus was dead.

'It is finished,' he said and I thought that was it. 'The pressure is relieved. Now we watch for the regeneration of life in the nerve fibres. There's a chance, one in four. We've done what anybody could have done, bar God. The boy has everything to live for, but they will never want him in the Navy again. He would not stand up to service life. He'll maybe break his heart about being pensioned off. Your Clunys are sailors in tradition from way back. He'll not take kindly to a desk job.'

'He need not take a desk job,' I began and then saw that this conversation was not on. The floor was the deck here and windows were ports. The stairs were the companionway.

We went home after a week or two and Fergus was up and about in a wheel chair by then and no danger now, only for the possible non-regeneration of tissue. The sister saw us off from the top of a flight of steps and the wheel chair teams were still playing polo, as if they had found themselves in some limbo with no escape, but to polo in invalid chairs for the rest of their lives and be very happy. I wondered if the sister knew that this was the last of the magic lantern slides. She was very kind. She and I had talked at length in long nights.

'He must expect to be chair-bound for a while. I have a feeling this case will turn out well. he'll be discharged to Derrycreevy House as soon as possible, but don't get big-headed about it. It's the fish in the river he's after, not his pretty young lady. He's fishing mad.'

Derrycreevy House had a wonderful reputation for youth and endeavour and victory. The Dean came to dinner as soon as I was home and Mrs. Cluny was our guest too. She warned us that we would not hear about Fergus's discharge till he walked in the front door. The Senior Service was like that, but she was very happy now. The out-going doctor, who was off to new Zealand, was very knowledgeable about spinal injuries. He gave us a great deal of information about them. He was looking forward to Fergus taking over as soon as might be, but wheel chairs were the devil.

'You have to keep on beyond all human endeavour in this

type of damned case. Leave off your crutches and your legs get lazy. Take to a wheel chair and your legs pack up – and you're chair bound. I think that there are patients who never walk again, just because they give up fight. Any physio-nurse will tell you the same. Lie in bed and stay there for the rest of your life. You must keep trying. Your muscles are T.U.C. men. They go on strike and the next week you can't move at all . . . maybe never again, so you crawl on your belly like a snake and at last you may walk upright like a man . . . if you grovel in the dirt first.'

I dare say that the Lord got tired of my prayer, yet the Dean laughed at me. He was always somewhere about. I think he had taken over for Rohan where I was concerned. There was only one doubt now. Had the pressure been lifted soon enough? That was the crux.

I kept on with prayer and maybe God got tired of me knocking at the gates of heaven in the middle of the night.

'The big fish is the luck of Derrycreevy,' I said. 'Let no person be fool enough to catch him. He's the luck of Rohan's house and always will be.'

I maybe seemed to have lost interest in the regeneration of Derrycreevy, but this was not so. The work went on. There were curtains by Bagnall and carpets by Fayle. Uncle James came over one day with a van of sheepskin rug mats as a present and had a day's ferreting with Dinny and Michael. The sheepskin mats were wonderful on the parquet. The Arab stud had been founded at Cloncon and Maw was to be at the spring Horse Show. If I came to Cloncon, I could have a bath with bath salts, in boiling water. I could flush with impunity. I could turn a switch and see the world created. A brave new world. The pity was that Violet, his new ferret bitch, had bitten Uncle James. He was light on his left rear. He had intended her as a present for Dinny and Michael, but she wouldn't do for them at all, at all. They would have to keep Tiger, who was as tame as a kitten, God bless his little white soul.

The Dean took me to task after a while, a sheep dog after a foolish lamb.

'We all know what will be, will be, Ann, Little Cat. Life goes on. We trust that the operation was a success. One day Himself will come running for you, but not yet. Don't ask too much. This sort of situation takes infinite patience.'

I confessed to him that I was disappointed. By now, surely Fergus should be free of the wheel chair. Instead, he was just another such man as the ones that had played polo, falling over and getting up again and going on with life.

His legs were still useless.

'They warned you, lassie,' said the Dean.

'The breaking of the telephone lines in the body is a grievous thing lassie,' he said. 'It takes a long time till you and he will play tennis again. If the lines are down for good, you'll be marrying a disabled man for your life and his. It's my duty to ask you to look at the full picture. He can be crippled, maybe for ever and want expert nursing. You must be told it. I do not think that anybody has dared to tell you that Fergus may never be able to beget your children.'

Here was the block-buster at last. I had somehow to know it . . . I heard it for the first time, when I thought that the recovery might be slow. He had had such virility once, but maybe . . .

My thoughts were eggs that had been put into a liquidator, spun to anonymity, the destruction of everything of the future. Finality from a fresh brown egg.

There had to be a making of a dynasty for Derrycreevy. Fergus could not come off the surgical spinal baggage chute, that shot out results like luggage. Fergus could never have become a half-man, damaged beyond any hope of fertility. Paralysis and all the rest of it was only a cover for the crunch. I thought of Derrycreevy and its dynasty and its inheritance. I could see Fergus trying to cope with the practice in a wheel chair, but modern medicine would smash such a man into comminution. There were secret nerves, that I had not even known. I had never known that everything might have been lost . . . love and the physical beauty of loving . . . and the mechanism of controlling the wastes of the body . . . the shameful childishness, when a person reverted to babyhood and indignity. Not for Fergus, never, never, never.

I had built up my dream of chivalry. I saw it crash down. I saw the whole disaster for what it was. Maybe I had seen Fergus take on the practice with a great heroism, but it was not like that. I knew beyond doubt that the end might be bad . . . past bearing. God help me! I pitied the heiress of Strawberry Hill on her wedding night. It was the end of my dreams for Derrycreevy, if Fergus was to be denied all loving for ever. If he could never be a father, then what had we, but a lifetime of brother and sister?

'I'm sorry, Dean Langdon. I was too greedy in my prayers. Put Fergus in the balance and put Derrycreevy against him, and he denied fatherhood and me to choose. I'd pick Fergus, no matter what comes out of it. I'd let them all go and Derrycreevy too – Annie and Sarah and Dinny and Aunt Bessie. I'd let the whole world go just for Fergus, my brother.'

Maybe I wanted to be God? I hoped for four strong sons. I wanted Fergus walking again, a whole man. I wanted children in Derrycreevy again. I wanted to bear his children. Fergus Cluny's for Gorse Hill sailors too. Then, more than that. I wanted Fergus to be Cluny, my husband, but also to be Rohan all over again.

'Hear this! Hear this! Cluny is come home again!' and, 'Where is my dam? and the glory for two great houses . . .' And soon I might be waiting in the warm bed with my arms out to him.

Nurse Geraldine Fitzgerald called to see me and said that Dean was a right old fool to have frightened me out of my wits.

'Did he have no knowledge that the nervous system in medicine dealt in years and not in days?'

'We have this one patient alive and well,' she said. 'And God be praised. Nerves will heal, if you give them half a chance. But Fergus must have confidence in himself. The Dean is just going round chattering like an old woman of something he knows nothing about. Don't make an invalid out of Fergus, for he's coming home and they hope he'll mend. We'll want a deal of patience. Can't you see the psychological bomb you have in this one case? This bloody dynasty of doctors in Derrycreevy! There's another dynasty in Gorse Hill and one versus the other. It's all moved out of sanity. The Brain Man lifted the pressure, so what went wrong? Has Fergus to be a second-class citizen, because somebody starts a scare? I refuse to start a scare. The pressure was lifted and God isn't vindictive. This I believe. Bring it all out in the open and say it. Fergus is still in the wheel chair, when he might have been walking, so he gets the wind up. We don't actually know it, but suppose it's so? He finds that maybe he's impotent. It's common enough in this sort of man. The question is between everybody. Was the pressure not released in time, your man could stay a second-class citizen for the rest of his life, when there's nothing wrong with him but funk.'

She went on . . .

'A person in the cloud can't see the su, but a person in the sun can see the whole of creation. Can he or can't he? People will look sideways at him . . . and I don't mean can he manage the bloody wheel chair. Give him self-respect. Give him confidence. Give him love, Ann. Give him non-demanding love. Wait, wait, wait, wait . . . and pray as you never prayed before.'

Of course it all went wrong. Somewhere along the road home to Derrycreevy, Fergus learned the secret, that I had never told him, not wanted him to know yet. I had MONEY. Was I not the heiress of an anonymous benefactor? No longer was I the poor little waif, who had eaten bread and jam on people's doorsteps. I was an heiress in my own right.

All I wanted was a man to step in Rohan's shoes and take over Derrycreevy. Derrycreevy was perhaps the love of my life.

So Fergus arrived in the wheel chair, changed from the old Fergus. True enough I wanted a Master for Derrycreevy, but it was better, if he did not know it. He was quite certain from the start, as soon as he heard it, that he wanted nothing to do with an heiress.

Perhaps Constance Peppard had never known what the marriage bed entailed, but I came from a different generation. I also had now found out what a spinal paralysis could do to a man. Fergus himself knew what the true issue was. I did not discuss it with him. It sounds unlikely that we should not talk about the reality of it at first, but we did not. All I knew was that I had been too hungry in my demands for the future. I had a fist in a jar, and filled it too full and maybe I could never escape. Maybe I was a prisoner, unless I let Fergus go?

So Fergus was home in Derrycreevy and he seemed no different from all the brave young men, who played polo in the fields and laughed, if they fell over. It broke my heart, when I found him in difficulties, jumbled up in furniture, waiting to be rescued . . . a prisoner in the garden in a skiddy patch with spinning wheels . . . down in the town of Ballyboy with the battery run out.

Then one day, he did speak of it, all that the Dean had told me and more. He was brutally frank and I cowered in front of him, said I did not care. Then he came to the crunch. He had heard I was an heiress. Why had I not told him? There was a good chance that he himself had been disinherited, by machine-gun fire, third world guerrillas fighting out of the dark. But now, he had agreed to try to do the practice till a new MAN could be found for it. Then he must be on his way. Never would he allow me to tie myself to a cripple.

I spoke my heart to him. I remember telling him that Derrycreevy House could go to the devil.

'It's you I love, Fergus.'

'It seems that we may never be able to love,' he said
sharply. 'Just bad luck . . . just one of those things. Yet I love
you in the same old way. I'm you and you're me, ever will be.
I dream of you at night and spend myself in the same old
way. I don't believe it's true. It can't be all gone, just because
I can't stand any more . . . can't walk to you and take you in
my arms. It can't all have vanished . . . not such a love as I
had for you, but it seems it's possible.'

So I was back at my foolish prayers again. I wanted
Fergus and into the scales I threw my whole life and the rest
of my world. Children had no part in my demands, none.

Fergus went for a hospital report and it was good . . .
good. . . good, reflexes returning to normal. His nerves
showed regeneration. Yet still he paddled about the house in
the wheel chair and lifted his legs to the steps by dint of using
his hands, one by one, foot by foot.

The specialist said that the time limit had nearly run out.
Six months and no better. If that happened, you drew the
line and wrote 'FINIS'. He was very sorry, but that was that.

The Norfolk farmer did not know what sort of woman I
was. Perhaps a brother-sister relationship would satisfy me
but there were tiresome nursing details that would be
necessary. I must understand it in full.

Then the "new doctor" was away for new Zealand within
weeks and no other locum available. Fergus was eager to
help as best he could, till a MAN was found. Easily he could
see patients in the old dispensary. He could be ferried round
the visiting list in the car, with one of us to push him in the
chair, but the cover was totally inadequate. For all our
efforts, Fergus knew he was inadequate and the thought
finished him and I could not see what we could do. He
resented being helped. maybe there were times when he
hated me, because I could walk and run.

God knows we all tried to help and it was probably the
worst thing we could do. One of us was always in attendance

at his surgeries and the patients liked him. He had the quick wit and all the humanity of a sailor. He saw to it that he listened to troubles and maybe they all took him as a super Dr. Kildare, on T.V. What did the wheel chair mean to such a hero? Could he not take a baby into his arms and hush its crying? Was it not himself, who knew when a cup of tea from the kitchen helped. There were old men who remembered his father and he found time to talk about those times. He was all set to be the best physician ever, if his legs walked again. He liked best to take the chair on his own round, maybe on a Sunday, when time hung slow, and call on the lonely ones, who sat from one week to the next.

'You can talk to yourself, Ann. The walls won't answer. After a time, I think these people are in a kind of cruel prison. I don't mind if I have to listen. Who am I to pick and choose the heroics of surgery? It's as much in the practice of medicine to listen.'

So we scraped through a few weeks and still his legs were powerless, but he held the practice on the ground without anything awful in the way of disaster. He even delivered a baby one night and I thought that maybe he came to life again, when the baby slid out like the fish in the pool . . . out on the draw sheet. I was in attendance and Nurse O'Brien and it was all probably illegal but it went well. he got the name for skilled maternity, because the baby seemed dead and he revived it, with his mouth pressed over its mouth and breathed confidence, not fear.

We were looking for trouble and I knew it, but he performed miracles in Ballyboy, he working against odds, that would have terrified most men. It goes to say we all worked for him. We all wanted it to come right, when it could never come right.

I had written off my demands for a family. If it was not to be, I had pushed it out of my mind, yet we were on edge with each other. maybe he was beginning to hate me, or maybe I imagined it.

'Can't you see I don't have to be pushed round like a bloody baby in a pram? God, Ann! I'm sorry, but I have to try to go under my own sail. I can't even try to go from A to B, but you're all in a rush to help me, like a bloody infant. I have to be picked up and my nappies changed and be pushed out again, helpless against a lot of do-gooders, who don't know when a man wants to be left alone to go to perdition his own way.'

We were round the corner of the house from the river and I was furious with him suddenly.

It was a spring day and the oak trees were beginning to bud. The ash trees were budding too, more black than my hair . . . so he had just told me and I was not far from hating him. It had all gone on too long and we were not going to win and I disliked the top naval surgeon, who had spoken so kindly to me, when I went across to see him personally at the hospital last week.

'I appreciate how much attention you have given to this chap, Miss Rohan. I would tell you never to give up. I have worked in this sort of surgery all my life and seen the odd miracle. This boy is written off by my colleagues now. The time has elapsed and still he has no promise in his loins . . . no promise in his muscles to climb mountains, but always I say to you: count in years, not in weeks. I have seen the deaf hear and the lame walk. There is a higher court than the medical profession. 'There are more things in heaven and earth, Horatio!' Give us more time . . . as much as might cover a mustard seed on a digital clock. This man still dreams of you and possesses you in his dreams and mark that, Ann. Take courage.'

The day was as clean in my mind as a new-minted coin in the golden light through the oak trees.

'Very well then. You can take yourself home quite easily. I'm going across the river and up the hill,' I said huffily. 'I want to be alone.'

'I'm sorry, Ann.'

'Of course, you're not sorry. You don't give a damn.'

I had lost patience with him and I hated myself for it. That morning we had had a letter from the medical committee, saying that they had found a young man, who would be willing and eager to take over the practice. As from the next quarter date, Surgeon Lieut. Cluny could relinquish his locum tenens and his efforts in filling a gap had been laudable. Now he could resign and rest fully and, doubtless, he might improve with time. The incoming doctor might choose to take the bungalow and the new surgery . . . It was all for decision in the near future.

I raised my nose an inch in the air and shot the brakes of the wheel chair to CLOSED. I just walked away from him at last, towards the fisherman's bridge. I put out a hand on the cable rail and felt the swing of the boards under my feet, remembered in that second how Rohan had chivvied us children about the maintenance of the planks and the cables.

I must see to that bridge tomorrow without fail.

Mea culpa! Always it had been our fault. Tomorrow I would keep faith. Out in the centre it was a deep drop to the water . . .deep water that bubbled and surged and foamed at the top of the weir. It happened quickly but I shall never forget the sequence of the disaster. One, two, and the board cracked and split apart. Three four, the cable sneaked round an ankle and held it fast. Five six, the bridge out from under me and the big stone in the waterfall caught my temple. I screamed as I fell, but the water cut off all sound. The cable held me suspended.

I breathed in a great deep breath of bubbling tossing spume. I tried to cry for help, but there was no hope of it. I took in great breaths of spinning tossing water. There was no hope of anybody hearing me, no hope of the cable releasing my ankle. I made an effort to rear myself up and come to the rope. I tried to cry out to Fergus but I knew there was nothing left for me to do. I was going to die thus . . . on this friendly fisherman's bridge, where I had played so many

times. My brains were dulling and my strength almost gone.
The blood was pounding in my ears and last of all, I recalled
the monkey's paw. Did one have all one's life flash past in
drowning? I clutched at the slippery hard stones of the weir
and the weed came away under my nails and then I went
deep again, breathed in the water and my fight over. In that
last moment, I thanked God for the mercy he had shown me
in life. I was too late repentant for asking so much. The lights
flashed once and went down and last of all was my prayer for
Fergus.

'Restore him, oh, God! To happiness, to happiness,
happiness and perfection.

'Restore him to perfection and love, this above all.'

Maybe I stood before Him as I uttered it. I don't know. It
was uttermost dark. I heard about it later and I think it
possible that I might have been standing at the final
judgement.

Dinny had been working in the garden and Annie taking
in the clothes. My scream had fetched them all, even Fergus
in the wheel chair. Dinny and Annie and Michael had run
for the bridge. I was hanging over the drowning hole and no
movement out of me by now. They could none of them swim
and they screamed for Fergus. He had moved the chair to the
river, but it was turned on its side. He was scrabbling about
in the ivy under one of the oak trees. He was dragging his
way through the spring growth. He was climbing up the ivy
of a great trunk and making a few steps towards the bank. He
was standing erect and their cries loud to him.

'She's caught by the rope under the fall. For God's sake,
get her out. We can't swim. Michael went in and half
drowned himself. He's in the shallows below, nigh dead. I'm
going to try to make it now, but I can't swim . . .'

'Mr. Fergus flung himself on the air and it bore him up.'

I shall never forget the description of it afterwards.

'His feet moved under him. He fell and picked himself up.
Then his feet moved under him by the will of God. He came

to the bank of the river and then he was gone like an arrow
. . . the power fully restored to him. He sheared that black
depth as a knife would and then Herself in his arms and the
rope free.'

They were to tell of the miracle in unison and it knitted
into a great plait of praise.

'He brought you over the river to us and we lifted you up
and you very sick from the water. Sure the river had taken
possession of you, but he wouldn't let you go. He put his
mouth down on yours and he searched all heaven for you . . .
and then you breathed once and then again and then once
more.'

'He was stooping down to talk to you,' Michael said, and
Michael like a drowned rat himself.

'After a while, it came to us that he was walking and the
clothes sticking to his back and he trying to make nothing of
what he had done. You opened your eyes after a while and
you smiling at him, as if it was nothing you had had except a
sweet dream. You asked him when he had started to walk
again and that took a start out of him. Then he said and we'll
never forget what he said,

"Now thank we all our God!"''

That was where the fable always ended and many times it
was to be told in the years to come and there was never any
different ending: 'Now thank we all our God!'

'And that was what happened, as God is our Judge. We
never expect to see the like of it again, till the oak trees
walked from the wood of Derrycreeevy, over to Gorse Hill
House.'

CHAPTER EIGHT

The Glass Heiress

It was going to end happily, for all that it had seemed impossible. It is no good to go into all the medical investigations, not yet talk about how the mind is the master of the body, nor mention psychosomatic medicine, nor maybe how once a long time ago, there was a Man, who made the lame walk. It goes without saying that Fergus took on Rohan's practice. It is idle to describe the feverish preparations for our wedding. Maybe Cloncon took up its skirts and moved ten miles nearer to Derrycreevy and we were glad of it.

Gran had had a change of character. With the change in her house, she had taken a new lease of life. She had turned into a beloved grandmother, who might come visiting, like any ordinary relative might do. I think the stud of pure-bred Arab ponies woke her from her sleep of the years. She even looked different. She had taken to dressing up to come visiting. The paste diamonds had disappeared. They had obviously been put away in a drawer. She was still faithful to the glass brooch. She was never without it. She took to man-tailored suits and always a white cravat and always in the white cravat, the old glass brooch. It was her trade mark in the show ring . . . the glass, that matched her eyes and mine.

She had come back to life as I had done. There was no doubt that we were both very happy.

So one day Fergus and I were wed and now he accepted

the full time responsibility of a single-handed general practice in a remote Midland town. Near enough the time he was to leave for the church, he got an emergency call, phoned through from Annie at Derrycreevy, for he was at Gorse Hill.

Annie was on the phone. There was no time to waste, wedding or no wedding.

'It's Mr. Gallagher of Sandymount Lane.'

Mr. Gallagher had come drunk just once too often late for his dinner. Fergus told me about it later. As his wife then, I was in his full confidence and very proud of it.

'Anyhow it didn't leave me time to hang about. I had to answer the call. Gallagher was stretched out unconscious on his own hearthstone. Poor little Mrs. Gallagher just didn't realise her own strength. She apologised for not realising that it was Miss Ann's wedding day. She would never have done it for the world, if only she had remembered. Mrs. Gallagher took one look at the top hat and took in the grey tie and the tail coat and the striped trousers . . . the white carnation.'

'Glory to God! We have a real doctor in Ballyboy at last. I can see a great change coming for us all. Gallagher will have to behave himself from now.'

It was strange but true.

It is such things that weddings are made of, far more than panoply and pride. Only it reminded me of Fergus's twenty-first Birthday and of the absent ones. Rohan would have given me away and there would have been a tumbling about of all those happy boys and girls . . . and Mother and all of them gone now, but they were somewhere about and not far away. Officiallly, Derrycreevy was not haunted any more in the eyes of the Ballyboy people. Mother had come and fetched her loved ones away and put paid to the haunting of the ancient house. Still I heard them in the lonely times, when I missed them again and again. Very often, I could hear children, chuckling on the bank of the river, but it was likely the chuckling of the waters over the fall. Up in the nursery, I would walk in by the door and quietly find the rocking horse just come to the end of a gentle gallop, slowing back into stillness. In the wind, I heard their voices, as I have always heard them. It was getting less and less, as the years went by. They were going farther and farther away. I knew that soon they would leave me to Fergus's care and come no more and I was sorry for it, but I knew that was how it would be . . . no more whispers on the stairs, no more doors that opened by themselves . . . no more doors that stood ajar, that had been tightly shut.

I would be gone to happiness in my marriage to Fergus. They would know I had no need of their watchfulness. Meanwhile it was time for me to go to the church as a bride.

It was strange how the practice stretched a finger out for Fergus and would not let him go free.

Any country G.P. will tell you the same. There's a kind of evil eye on some urgent calls.

So it was with us, Fergus was almost late for his own wedding. He reached his seat in the church, just as I arrived in great pomp at the porch with my retinue. I had the village grapevine from the sexton one moment after I entered the church porch.

'Take it aisy, Miss Ann. The bridegroom is only in the front pew this second, with Mr. McCarthy. It's a dead heat. They haven't had time to get to the chancel rails yet and the organist is holding back on the Mendelssohn for a bit, to let us all calm down. Dr. Fergus had an urgent call to see to, and he went as he was, in his swallow tails and grey cravat and grey topper and all. I dare say Mrs. Gallagher thought she had sent for the Angel Gabriel by mistake.'

I sorted it out in quick whispers. It seemed that Mrs. Gallagher of Sandymount Lane had chosen my wedding day to turn like a rat on Gallagher and good luck to her. The story was filtering through the church like a genie. The choir had it. The organist had it. The bell ringers had it. I had it myself when I arrived, the bridesmaids giggled.

It seemed that Mrs. Gallagher had had mind set on attending our wedding and Gallagher had come home late and drunk with it. It was the last straw of a very big straw-stack. She had not realised the strength in her arm. She had levelled him on his own hearthstone. Then she had thought she had killed him. The eldest child had gone running to Derrycreevy for the doctor to come quick.

Mrs. Gallagher had looked at Fergus when he arrived and she had not recognised his grandeur.

'Dear God! We have a real doctor in Ballyboy,' she had said. 'Wouldn't the look of him put the fear of God in anybody?'

It was a strange message for a bride to get at the church door. I imagine that Women's Lib might have arrived at Sandymount Lane and indeed Fegus proved himself well able to steer Gallagher cottage for the future.

As for me, the wedding was the same as all weddings, with everything going wrong at the last moment. First the wedding cake had arrived late from Oakley's bakehouse, but when it came, it was splendid. I gaped at it in the dining-room, my mind filled with the memory of hot doughnuts, bubbling in a cauldron of fat. I thought of all the slices of ham I had had from the prongs of a carving fork . . . slices of home-baked Limerick ham, when I had pains in my stomach with hunger and old Oakley had caught the look in my eyes. This was my wedding day and he had given me an elegant cruet as a gift. It will always have pride of place on my table. The old man is in his grave long ago, but he understood the need of a child in big trouble. He was one of the people who had provided the warming pan for the ladybird, when her children were all gone. There were so many people I owed.

The sexton was at my elbow.

'The organist is ready to start the Mendelssohn now, Miss Ann. Mr. Fergus is at the rail. God go with you both! If only

Rohan had lived to see this day, he'd have been the proud man.'

All spring was filling the Church with thanksgiving. There were flowers in the window embrasures and my hand was in his . . .

But back to Derrycreevy House, where all the drama was happening, though maybe I did not realise it. They had said that the bridegroom was out on an urgent visit. They said he would be late at the church. Grandmother had left already, a plate of fashion in the tailored black suit, but she had left her cravat on the hall seat and her green brooch stuck in it. There was panic in the house till somebody had taken it into safe keeping.

I fussed with her a bit about leaving it, when she came back to the reception.

'You're a dear girl to worry about me,' she said. 'You looked after me when I was in trouble. I've left that brooch to you . . . may as well know it now. You always called it a Christmas cracker emerald. How will it suit you to be left a Christmas cracker gem in my will, my Glass Heiress? I've always called you that, you know . . . my Glass Heiress . . . poor little Ann!'

Desmond McCarthy had brought it to me later, for she had forgotten it again. It was the first time he had had a good look at it.

'So that's how she did it?' he said almost to himself. 'The cunning old vixen.'

He and I had got marooned in a corner, the way one does at such functions. He bent his head to mine.

'You told me she had given up the paste diamonds, after you left Cloncon,' he said. 'It all becomes clear. She wore no jewels today except her wedding ring and this emerald and then she was careless about it, not once but twice. She told you it was willed to you and maybe she joked about Fortnum's crackers. That's her all over. It was one of the

Strawberry Hill jewels . . . don't know how I missed it, as everybody else missed it in its camouflage. The diamonds were real too. This emerald was the best of all the Strawberry Hill jewels. Can't you see it even now?'

I shook my head and murmured something about Fortnum's crackers again and he laughed outright at that, so that people turned round to look at us.

'She gave up wearing the paste diamonds and soon after the will was made, making you the legatee to an anonymous fortune. Longman, Longman, Longman, Jones and Longman, had had the paste diamonds and translated them into cash . . . a great deal of cash. They had been hidden out on grimy fingers and grubby scarves . . . hidden out in Glen Leven too, God knows how. She took her fortune out of Strawberry Hill and she kept it intact. She didn't let her husband waste it away. She set it by against real need. It seems she saw that you were in real need and you were like the girl she remembered in the portrait. The ones that stole the furniture away were not the only smugglers, but most of that went to ashes. She saw what you did for her in Cloncon and she knew herself in debt to you. The gold you found had set her up, but you were in trouble still and she owed you . . . and loved you . . . she had seen you sloshing about in wellingtons, saw your hands turn to lobsters, saw you cut by your friends, because you were lifting herself out of the God-awful mess she had made of her own life and her family's lives too. She saw you growing to womanhood and no chance of a future for you . . . not a hope in hell. She decided to make you the heiress, that she should have been. She had made nothing of herself, but sorrow . . .'

He held out the cravat to me with the brilliant green stone pinned in it.

'Here it is then. The Kipling emerald, that has been missing for years. She's very careless with it, to have left it behind again.'

I took the cravat and examined the emerald and wondered

how we could all have been fooled, but the large paste diamonds too that had been on her hands, when she mixed the horse's hot bran mash . . . and us fooled by the grubby handkerchiefs and the shawls that the woolly dog inhabited . . . by the sheer carelessness of her, that she could leave the emerald behind twice in one day. I was still in my bridal gown and the guests seemed to be leaving. Fergus was looking everywhere for me and my train was twenty feet long. I wondered how I could dispose of it, if I had to run and indeed it seemed that I must run.

'I must say goodbye,' I cried to Desmond and he put out his hand to stop me. 'She's almost at the front gate.'

'Remember the terms of that will,' he said soberly. 'Don't make a fool of yourself. You must not pry into the identity of the benefactor.'

'That be damned!' I said, for I had seen the Cloncon car was down the avenue on its way home and I had not said goodbye to her. I had her cravat and the Kipling emerald in my hand. I made a great bundle of my train and I ran like a hare, down the avenue straight for the gate, between the oak trees, just as if I was running away.

'Come back,' called Desmond. 'For Christ's sake, come back. You're going to ruin everything. You're supposed never to know. Can't you remember you'll make it all null and void? You'll be penniless again. Don't be a fool. She could do it too, if you were ass enough to cross her.'

'Come back!' I called. 'Come back!'

She had the car halted outside the gates and the window screwed down. She looked at me through a lorgnette, that she must have retrieved from some old drawer.

'What is it, child?' she asked me.

I stood by the open window, my train bundled in my left arm and her cravat held out to her in my right hand and the emerald like the green eye of the little yellow God, stuck up in it.

'You forgot it again. You'd have gone off without it. You

left your cravat on the hall seat. You left the glass brooch.'

'The glass brooch?' she said and pretended to be surprised.

She took the cravat out of my hand and no notice of my trembling. She chided me for bundling up my train in such an unlady-like way. She slung the cravat round her throat and took infinite care to get it to sit correctly under the clear-cut jaw. Then she stuck the emerald into the cloth with a fine carelessness.

'I could have collected it another day,' she said. 'There's no need for all this fuss.'

'I'd never let you leave without bidding you goodbye,' I said. 'Or thanking you.'

'For what?' she shot off at me.

'For providing the warming pan for a ladybird who flew away home. There were many people helped in making a warming pan. I've maybe got round to thanking them, but I find I maybe never thanked you . . . and I owe you . . . and always will owe you.'

'You owe me nothing but goodbye to you. You're a fine gel and good fortune to you and your man.'

And that was all.

I watched the car disappear up Gallows Hill and I wanted to weep, but there was no time for it. Fergus and Desmond had found me and it is extraordinary what a mess two sane men can make of a bridal train. Desmond was too intent in trying to whisper legal advice to me.

'Not a word to her either now or later, only to Fergus here and he knows it already. The Czarina never wants it known and maybe we honour her wish.'

'We honour her,' I said. 'So we honour what she wishes . . .'

And that is how it has been and it is enough about a wedding. I had lived my life the best way I could. Somewhere I lost my happiness and found it again, when the odds had been all against my doing it. Sometimes, it seemed

to me that time had come round in a full circle and it has all
happened again.

Derrycreevy has returned to being the house I
remembered, but perhaps with some of the characters
replaced in the cast of whatever play fate puts on. Fergus and
I inhabited the master-bedroom now and he had taken to
being very like the "old Doctor" in the patients' eyes. Then
joyfully I was with child. Rohan, my first son, was born after
a year, and was on the way to being spoilt by everybody,
when the second son, Fergus, arrived. Fergus senior and I
loved each other with an intense passion, that burnt us with
flame. We were both hungry for children. We were in love
with loving and we had both known a strange childhood,
that had seen how easily children can be lost. In another
while, our first daughter came and we called her "Constance
Peppard" and the Czarina was so pleased that she said 'she
could now depart in peace.' We laughed at her, but maybe
we knew what she meant. Maybe she had come full circle
too. I think she had.

'You're greedy for children, Little Cat,' she said to me, but
you have two houses, greedy for children too . . .' and so it
went on. Maybe we replaced all the empty spaces that
remained. I knew that the children seemed the same as we
had always been in the old days. They had only to cross the
river and go over the hill to see Grandmother Cluny, who
watched for their coming.

'Be careful of Baby Con on the bridge, now.'

It was a bridge with a legend in the annals of Ballyboy.
Maybe there was a miracle in it too. I shall never think
otherwise.

So the days slipped into years and time passed smoothly
and Fergus going grey at the temples. The practice was the
same as it had always been and the surgery or maybe the
kitchen a sanctuary for people in trouble or maybe sorrow or
need or sickness and nobody turned away. Dinny still
guarded the front steps and the gold watch shone pride out of

the sun. Michael still held the front gates and perhaps against any evil, that flew by night or by day.

Aunt Bessie was the happiest of anybody I ever knew. She had a new family, just as I had and she was the best loved person in the whole place. Always she seemed to carry the youngest one in her arms and look after the rights of the oppressed against the elders of the nursery.

'Now you know, Miss Baby, that ships are for sailing . . . and not for pretending they're horses and banging them against the wall for a six-foot fence to jump.'

'Oh dear!'

Many years later it was a cold night. It had been a cold year and maybe it was January or February or March. I could not work it out when the telephone rang at my side of the bed.

It was nothing I could ditch with an aspirin and 'call again in an hour, if she's not better.'

'It's Mrs. McCreedy,' I said to Fergus, who was sleepy at my side. 'Geraldine says she's right for her dates. She's almost full. You said you wanted to deliver her yourself, so it's time to go.'

'Oh! God. Why is it always the wee small hours?' Fergus groaned.

It was all happening again, the night visit. It meant the white polo-necked sweater, double knit. It meant the studded walking shoes, for there was light-frosted snow on the ground.

'Only for you, Honey,' Fergus said. 'I'd be manning one of Her Majesty's ships, and freezing to death. It's far better on my own patch and on yours. Don't want me ever to change to an admiral . . .'

Then he was gone and I knew that Michael would have the kit on board and the car ready, for I had alerted him.

I switched on the electric blanket on the bed, switched on the electric kettle, got out the bottle of sherry and squat bottle of Bovril. It would be ready for him, when he came home, maybe in one hour or in four. I thought of him, as I waited and maybe prayed for Mrs. McCreedy. I knew birth pains by now . . .

It was only one hour later, when the light on the landing slitted the bedroom door and Fergus was in the room, half trying not to disturb me, but hoping he would. These were secret golden moments, when life could be very sweet to us both. His whisper reached me, loud and clear.

'Hear this! Hear this! Where are my pretty chickens and their dam? The chickens are excused by reason of the lateness of the hour. The dam will be waiting for me, always faithful. Signal reads, loud and clear. Cluny is home from sea . . . repeat Cluny is home from sea . . .'

Cold from the night outside, he came to my arms and I held him to my breast with a great thankfulness. This was the way of it, this great joy in my heart. It had all ended in happiness, that had been meant from the beginning of time.

Cluny was home from sea. Tomorrow the news would spread by the grapevine that Mrs. McCreedy had had a fine son in the night. There was a new life started on its way. God was in his heaven. All was right with the world . . .